Chills at
Her Living Cry

Novels by Kevin St. Jarre

Absence of Grace

Aliens, Drywall, and a Unicycle

Celestine

Paris, California

The Book of Emmaus

The Twin

Chills at Her Living Cry

KEVIN ST. JARRE

Encircle Publications
Farmington, Maine, U.S.A.

Hardcover ISBN 13: 978-1-64599-573-9
Paperback ISBN 13: 978-1-64599-572-2
Ebook ISBN 13: 978-1-64599-574-6

Library of Congress Control Number: 2024948566

Editor: Cynthia Brackett-Vincent

Book design and cover design by Deirdre Wait
Cover photograph: *The Horse Trainer*, 1899, Felix Thiollier

Published by:

Encircle Publications, LLC
PO Box 187
Farmington, ME 04938

http://encirclepub.com
info@encirclepub.com

For my little sister, Christine. I love you.

1

◇◇◇◇◇

PARIS
1922

At twenty-four years old, I was a reporter for the *Boston Examiner*, living in Paris. Things had improved, after the tough times that immediately followed the war. Actually, it hadn't been my original intention to move to France. I had been sent by the newspaper, from my post in England, to Paris. At first, I was not enthusiastic about the change, because I worried that France would be filled with nothing but snooty Frenchmen, speaking a language I hardly spoke, and looking down their noses at me.

As it turned out, I enjoyed Paris a great deal. My American salary went further, but more importantly, it was the place to be. Paris had more people who were not originally born there than any other city in Europe. Even on the trip over from England, from New Haven to Dieppe, I had met the ferry's energetic pastry chef. He was a diminutive, energetic fellow from the Annam region of Indochina, and he spoke more about Communism than he did about pastries.

It was truly an inspiring time to be in Paris. There were artists, writers, intellectuals and those who fancied themselves as such, photographers, musicians, and some who were even dabbling in filmmaking, although I'm sure they thought they were serious artists as well.

The rich, also, were moving into Paris. Most were not creative themselves, but certainly liked to associate with those who were. Some wealthy did what they had long done; they became the patrons of artists. The affluent newcomers moved into the 9th arrondissement mostly, while many of the artists and writers found themselves flats in the 5th, and some of those without running water.

Paris was a cultural stew and, for a story, I began researching a people from within France, about whom I was only vaguely familiar. Honestly, even after I had investigated the story, I still didn't understand much more about them. Called the *gens des Marais*, and by a variety of other less polite names such as *Cagot*, I came to learn that there was more invented about them than actually known.

The origin of the Cagots was unclear. Some claimed they were descendants of the Visigoths, or of the Moors who had vanquished them. Perhaps both were true. One of the more outlandish stories was that they were all descended from the carpenters who built the cross of Christ.

The Cagot had been persecuted for centuries, and although they had historically been found in southwestern France and northern Spain, in recent decades they had largely dispersed across the country. When I mentioned the idea of such a story to my colleagues, one told me about an old man, living right there in Paris, who was himself a Cagot. He said he would see if he could get me an appointment to meet him.

A few days later, I went over to meet seventy-nine year old Alcide Chrétien. Alcide's flat was in a building one-removed from the corner of Boulevard Bourdon, on Rue Mornay. It being a nice day, I decided to walk from my tiny place on Rue Valette. I chose a route that would take me by the university, and maximize my chances of seeing young women down that way. I then crossed Pont de Sully, and the island of course, turning onto Rue de Sully and passing the stables of *Gendarmerie Nationale-Garde Républicaine*. All I could see was a high tan-brick wall running the length of the street, with the small, arched windows on the ground floor, each one seemed to mark a stable. The air was rich with the sweet scent of horse manure, and it certainly reminded me of my grandparents' New England farm.

When I reached Alcide's building, I looked up, and then across the intersection and canal, before taking a deep breath and entering. Climbing those flights of stairs, I wondered at the challenge they must be for an old man. After he opened the door for me, I introduced myself, saying, "Monsieur Chrétien, I'm Robert Markie. I'm the correspondent from Boston. Our mutual friend said you had agreed to see me." All I saw in the face of old Alcide was sadness, and wisdom born of it.

Alcide was short, and his face was deeply lined. The point of his stubble-covered chin was surely closer to his nose than it had been in his youth, and he had virtually no lower earlobes to speak of. This characteristic made me wonder if he, as the legends said of the Cagots, had webbed toes as well. Those who had persecuted them had forced them to wear patches with the insignia of a goose's red foot.

His eyes were a dull greyish-blue, and decades of being in the sun had baked his skin hard.

After I introduced myself, Alcide silently turned and walked away, neither closing the door, nor inviting me in. I followed. The furnishings in the flat were poor. One chair was handmade of unfinished, greying wood. The place smelled of cloves. He didn't pause as we walked through the flat and went right out onto the surprisingly large terrace, with nothing but open sky above and, along with a small table and chairs, it was crowded with potted plants. Some were as tall as I. Going to the far end, I could see the canal again, and the rooftops all around.

"It's a lovely spot. Thank you for seeing me," I said.

"Sit," Alcide said, and we did.

"Thank you. As I hope you've been told, I'd like to tell the story of the gens des Marais," I said.

"That is not a nice way to say it. I never lived in the marshes anyway. I live closer to Le Marais now than I ever have," Alcide said, thumbing over his shoulder.

It took a moment before I understood what he meant, but then I smiled, and he nodded. Le Marais district of Paris was about a five-minute walk from this flat, on the same side of the river, although it was hardly a marsh.

"What should I call you, if not gens des Marais? Cagot?" I asked.

"What if you call me simply, 'Alcide'?"

Shifting in my seat, I asked, "And how should I refer to your people?"

"Whatever way you like, in your story. I can only tell you about me, not the people as a whole. What you decide to do with what I tell you is up to you," Alcide said.

"I see. So, perhaps we should begin. Where were you born?" I asked, pulling my paper from my bag.

"We should start much farther along. Men are more interesting than babies," Alcide said.

I placed the paper on the table, and studied him for a moment. He looked back, unblinking, but with his lips moving, as if he were silently talking. It appeared Alcide Chrétien had a tale he wanted to tell, and he did not seem to care if it was the story I had come to collect.

"Fine. Will you start with today? Or perhaps a bit farther back?" I asked.

"Do not take a tone," Alcide said.

"My apologies. Please," I said.

"When I was seventy-one, I took a new job…" Alcide began to say.

"You took a job at that age?" I asked.

"The war had begun, and the young men knew they would have to go. Older men like me were being hired all over, because we knew farming, and remembered how to work hard," Alcide said.

"And this was in France?" I asked.

"Near Lyon. On the Arsenault farm, at the edge of Montagnat," he said.

"So, Arsenault is a family name, and Montagnat is a village?" I asked.

He paused, and asked, "You are not stupid, are you?"

"No, monsieur, I am not," I said, a bit insulted. While I didn't have fine clothes, I would have thought my vocabulary and grammar signaled that I was educated. My lack of familiarity with every hamlet and surname in France should not have been that much of an indictment.

"Good, because this is a complicated story, with bits that would shock an idiot. If you are feeble, you will not understand it," Alcide said.

"Go on," I said.

"I was hired on to work for Henri and Seraphine Arsenault. It was a small farm, northeast of Lyon and west of Geneva. One city was not closer than the other. There were the usual animals, such as chickens and goats, many cats, and two mares. An older one named

Bijou was a grey Ardennais, at least in part, and there was a beautiful bay named Esme," Alcide said.

"What did you do for them?" I asked.

"All that needs to be done on a farm. I could do it all. Especially easy when the majority of the animals are smaller, such as goats and chickens," Alcide said.

"It makes sense that bigger animals might be more work," I said.

"The largest farm I ever worked on had many cows, but even more work than those are pigs," Alcide said.

"Why pigs?"

"Picture a full-grown dairy cow. How fast do the really run? How much energy do they have?" Alcide said.

"And pigs are fast?"

"Pigs are quite fast, even when they weigh more than you! More stubborn as well, and pigs are very smart—as smart as dogs," Alcide said.

"Really?"

"Imagine if you had thirty dogs, all of them seventy kilograms or more, and they are all screaming and running, slick with manure, all very clever," Alcide said.

"I can imagine managing them would be a challenge," I said.

"Quite so," Alcide said.

"So, how many pigs did the Arsenaults have?" I asked.

"None," he said.

"Why did you bring them up?"

"We were discussing how much work different

types of farm animals are. I told you pigs are more of a
challenge than cows," Alcide said.

We stared at each other a moment, and then I asked,
"What was challenging at the Arsenault farm?"

"Well, at the Arsenault farm, it was easy work when
Henri was still there, and everyone seemed happy. I
think, for a while, even I was happy. They were both
expecting babies," Alcide said.

My brow furrowed. *Both expecting babies?* If he had
said that they were both expecting a baby, that would
have made sense. Henri and Seraphine were looking
forward to a child's arrival, but babies? "So, Seraphine,
was expecting twins?" I asked.

"Seraphine and Esme, the mare. They were due about
the same time. Henri had said that they needed me
especially because he would be leaving, and his wife and
mare were both in blood," Alcide said.

"In blood?" I asked.

"No, not in blood. Pregnant," Alcide said. "Are you
sure you know French well enough to do this?"

I blushed a bit. My parents had spoken French to
each other, but mostly English to us children. My
understanding of the language was better than my
speaking. I didn't answer his question, and instead I
asked, "There was no other help on the farm?"

Alcide's eyes narrowed a bit, and he said, "We will
talk about Olivier later."

I took notes, but so far, his account was starting out

like millions of other war stories. No one needed to be reminded. The war had ended only four years before, and the people who told their war stories in great detail were usually making them up.

Alcide stood, and walked back into the flat. This time I did not follow. He returned with a photograph, cigarettes, and matches. He placed the cigarettes and matches on the table, and handed the black and white photo to me. It was of a woman, slim in her black coat, with long sleeves and a high collar. Its hem went to the ground, but it was split in the back, and in the front, it was unfastened below her waist. She was running in the snow, with her boots visible. Her long dark hair was tied tight to her head, and in her right hand was a riding crop. She was chasing a dark-colored horse, and they were both running away from the photographer. Huge snowflakes were falling. Both the horse and the woman looked wild.

"Seraphine and the horse, Esme?" I asked.

Alcide shook his head. "This is Seraphine and Esme's foal, Elise." After he said it, his mouth set hard.

Looking at the photo, I asked, "Where are they now?"

"Listen to me. I will tell you," Alcide said, and he lit a cigarette. He offered one to me, and I declined. He took a deep puff of his cigarette and then he began to tell me about the Arsenault farm.

2

◇◇◇◇◇

MONTAGNAT
1914

Alcide got word of possible work from a man he passed on the road. They were about the same age, but he was walking the other way, likely headed to a job he had already secured. The two men didn't say much. They exchanged pleasantries, updates on work sought and work found, and the news that France was in the process of conscripting as many as 3,000,000 men for the coming defense of their land.

"The farm is not far. A way down the road," he said.

"How many cows are there?" Alcide asked.

"None, but horses and goats, and chickens," said the man.

"The name again?" Alcide asked.

"Arsenault. Henri is his name," the man said.

"Uncommon surname," Alcide said.

"They all went to Canada long ago. There are some in

Loiret, and some on the coast, but certainly few out this way," he said.

"I will go see," Alcide said.

Neither man said anything more, not even to share best wishes, and both resumed walking. When Alcide finally saw a house with a small barn, he put down his bag and straightened his shirt. He removed his hat, and swept his thinning hair back. Picking up his bag, he popped the hat back on. He didn't swing the bag up over his shoulder once more, but just carried it at his side. Alcide began calling out once he passed the first fence.

"Hello! Hello there!" Alcide said.

"Yes?" a man said, stepping out of the barn.

"Monsieur Arsenault? My name is Alcide Chrétien. I was told you might need a man here," Alcide said.

"Do you tire easily?" the man asked.

"I walked many miles to get here, and I can work right this minute," Alcide said.

"You have worked on a farm," the man said.

"Much of my life," Alcide said.

"Horse training? Husbandry?" the man asked.

"I was even a farrier, but long ago. And I can do light carpentry," Alcide said.

"And you're not a thief," the man said.

"Certainly not," Alcide said.

He stared at Alcide for a moment, and then said, "I am Henri Arsenault. You can sleep in the barn. Breakfast is early, and supper is late, but my wife Seraphine is a good cook. While I am still here working with you, your room and board will be your pay, but when I leave you will have more to do, and we will pay you what we can."

"When will you leave, monsieur?" Alcide asked.

"Call me Henri. I am not certain yet, but it will be soon," he said, and then looked toward the house.

Alcide also looked that way, and knew that Henri was likely more worried about those in the house than about what he was facing in the army.

Henri said, "You said you have been a farrier."

"I have."

"Was that a very long time ago?" Henri asked.

"I am quite a bit older, but I am still quite strong," Alcide said.

"I'm sure," Henri said, with a smile.

"Are you mocking me, Monsieur?" Alcide asked, using the formal 'vous'.

Henri's smile fell, and he said, "Not at all. And, please, as I said, call me Henri. I'm afraid we do not have time for the normal shift from being formal to familiar. You may stop using 'vous' as well. I'm just Henri. Alright?"

Alcide said, "I may slip at first."

"I'll forgive," Henri said, with only half a smile this time.

Alcide nodded, and looked him over. He seemed a nice, sturdy young man. "What would you like me to do first?" Alcide asked.

Henri said, "Why don't you put your bag in the loft?

Make yourself a place. Then, come down and find me."

Alcide went into the barn, climbed into the loft, and found it full of sweet, dry hay. He put his bag down and pulled an old blanket from it, which he lay upon the hay nearest his feet. After putting his bag on top of the blanket, he turned, climbed down the ladder. Alcide found Henri with the goats.

Henri said, "Are you thirsty? There is a pump, just there."

Alcide went over and pumped water into his hand, and wet his face. He pumped again, caught the ice-cold water with both hands, drank, and rubbed his face again. He came back to Henri and the goats, and said, "A deep well."

Henri smiled again, and Alcide thought he might not get used to a man who smiled so often.

"Come, I'll introduce you to the horses," Henri said.

They walked to the pasture where the mares were grazing, and both horses' heads came up at once.

"This is Bijou, and this is Esme," Henri said. "I think Esme has another forty days to go."

Alcide walked toward Esme, her belly hanging low.

"Careful. She has always kicked, and is even more temperamental now, I'm afraid," Henri said.

Alcide never slowed, nor did he give Esme a reassuring rub on the nose first. He walked directly to her flank, and put his hand on her side. Esme turned her head, and gave him a sniff, but did not take so much as a step. Alcide rubbed her belly.

"Careful now," Henri said.

Esme bent her head to the grass. Alcide turned back to Henri and said, "You do not have forty days. Maybe not even twenty. She has been in foal for 310 days, 320 days."

"We think so, too, about 310 days," Henri said.

"And you thought she would go 350 or more?" Alcide asked.

"She was a maiden mare. This is her first," Henri said.

"Monsieur, I think you have two weeks, three at most," Alcide said.

"I was hoping it would be longer. My wife is due soon as well. Unless you can tell if the doctor is wrong about her," Henri said.

"I have never been able to tell anything about women," Alcide said.

Henri laughed and said, "We're alike then."

"How so?" Alcide asked.

Henri's smile fell a bit, and then he said, "Nothing. Come, come meet Seraphine."

The men walked to the house, and Henri led the way inside. Alcide closed the door behind them, and removed his hat.

Henri called, "Seraphine, we have a guest."

She appeared, with her long hair tied neatly around the crown of her head, without a scarf to cover it. Wearing a white blouse, and skirt with a floral print, she had covered some of these with a worn and faded apron of cerulean blue. Her abdomen protruded so much that the apron, normally tied above her hips, was cinched beneath her heavy breasts.

"This is Monsieur Alcide Chrétien. This is my wife, Seraphine," Henri said.

"Monsieur Chrétien," she said.

"Please, call me Alcide, Madame," he said.

"Seraphine, then," she said, and Alcide nodded, wringing his cap a bit in his hands.

"Alcide will be working here, helping us," Henri said.

"Have you put your belongings in the barn, then?" she asked.

Alcide nodded.

"We can certainly use the help," Seraphine said with a smile.

"He says that Esme will foal in two weeks," Henri said.

"That soon?" she asked.

"No later than that," Alcide said.

"So, you know horses?" Seraphine said, moving to a small wooden chair. Sitting, she waved the men to join her at the table.

"Esme gave him no more than a sniff, and returned to grazing while he touched her belly," Henri said, as he moved to sit, patting Seraphine on her belly along the way.

"You're joking. I'm glad I wasn't watching. I would have been sure you would be kicked, or bitten," Seraphine said.

"Why do you keep a horse like that?" Alcide asked.

"She is Bijou's friend," Seraphine said. "I think sometimes that Esme is actually Bijou's horse."

"Does Bijou still work?" Alcide asked.

"Not as much as she used to, but she does still pull a cart when I need her to," Henri said, "Have you helped many mares to foal?"

"So many," Alcide said, and then couldn't help but glance at Seraphine's belly.

"Ah, don't worry. We have a midwife—her name is Madame Dubois—who will help me, and the priest, Père Benoit, will likely be here, too," Seraphine said.

"Maybe I will still be here," Henri said.

Seraphine's face became a bit pained, but she smiled through it, and said, "I hope."

"There was a neighboring house, with a barn, but I only saw chickens. I passed it on my way here," Alcide said.

"Jean and Claire Voisine's house, but Jean is already gone. He went to Paris," Henri said.

"Did they hire a man?" Alcide asked.

"Claire's daughter Suzanne, their only child, will help there. The girl is a hard worker. Is she sixteen years old now, Henri?" Seraphine asked.

"I think that's right," Henri said.

"She came home?" Alcide asked.

"She never left. Suzanne is a strong girl to work on a

farm, but she doesn't really speak. She does as she is told, and does her best, but she was never one that would be sent to a school. Suzanne doesn't have the head for it," Henri said. "I'm sure it's lonely for Claire."

"Is the girl mute?" Alcide said.

"I have heard her yelling at the chickens, but not with words. More like simple sounds, I'm afraid," Seraphine said.

"She gets angry at those birds, until she is using the axe, then she sort of coos to them. Perhaps in sympathy, or apology," Henri said.

"Apologize to chickens," Alcide said, and shook his head.

Seraphine's eyes narrowed, and she asked, "Do you ever consider the feelings of animals, Alcide?"

Alcide looked from her face to Henri's, and back again. He said, "With horses, very much so. And cows, too, I suppose, although a cow is an idiot compared to a horse."

"I see," Seraphine said.

Alcide looked around, and asked, "You don't have a dog?"

"He died in the spring," Henri said, and they both looked sad.

"Well, a good dog can make a man look like an idiot, and a dog is as feeling a creature as any. No farm should be without one," Alcide said.

"I agree with you," Seraphine said, "Did you have a

good dog once, Alcide?"

"His name was Callidus. I have never, nor will I ever, see the likes of him again. Black and white, fast as lightning, and so smart I bet he could have learned to read if we could have found a person smart enough to teach him," Alcide said.

"You said 'we.' You were married, then?" Henri asked.

Alcide paused, and then said, "I meant me and the dog."

There was a moment when no one spoke, until Seraphine asked, "Are you an educated man?"

Alcide shifted in his seat. "An educated farm worker?" he asked.

Seraphine tilted her head, and waited for an answer.

"I attended school for some time," Alcide said, as if confessing something, but then he added, "Nevertheless, I am not a dreamer. I am a hard worker."

"I have no doubt," Seraphine said.

Henri said, "Both of us can read as well."

Seraphine cleared her throat, and asked, "And what of goats and chickens?"

"What of them?" Alcide asked.

"What do you think of them?" she asked.

"Goats are not so much intelligent as they are... *rusée*," Alcide said, "And the smartest part of a chicken comes in a shell, hopefully once per day."

Henri chuckled, and then asked, "Do you have any questions of us?"

"Do you attend church?" Alcide asked.

"We had not in some time, but in recent weeks, we have begun again. The church nearby is Saint-Clair. You are welcome to come with us, if you like," Seraphine said.

"I do not attend," Alcide said.

There was a long pause, as if the Arsenaults were waiting for Alcide to say more, but Alcide sat quietly, as if there was nothing else to add.

Henri said, "I see. Any other questions?"

"Normally, it is only you two here, doing this work?" Alcide asked.

"Some days, there is a boy, Olivier, who comes. He does some work in exchange for a little loaf, or a couple of eggs, and then he leaves," Henri said.

"You know his family?" Alcide asked.

"We have never met them," Seraphine said.

"He simply arrived one day, just as you have. He asked if he could clean stalls or milk goats in exchange for food. Olivier is not very big, even for his age, so many things he cannot do, but he does enough," Henri said.

"He never eats with us. I have tried to have him stay, but he would rather take his food and go," Seraphine said.

Alcide said, "Perhaps he is sharing the food."

"He takes very little," Henri said. "I tried to follow him home twice. Once, I lost him in the forest, where the terrain becomes quite steep east of here. The second time, I was more careful, but he waited behind a tree and startled me. He wanted to know why I was following him, and I told him I did it out of concern. Olivier then told me there was no reason for concern, and asked me to never follow him again. I told him I would not. It hadn't been my idea anyway." Henri looked at Seraphine, who scowled back.

After a moment, Alcide asked, "So, should we get to it?"

"Of course," Henri said.

The men nodded at Seraphine, and headed outside. They went to the barn, and Henri said, "I'll feed the goats. Check Bijou's hoof, the left rear. She seems to be favoring."

Alcide said nothing, and went out to the large horse. He rubbed her nose a bit, and walked to her rear hoof, running his hand down her flank. Alcide patted that leg and she did nothing. With his back to her, he reached between his legs, and pulled on her hoof. If she had wanted to leave it down, there would have been little Alcide could do about it. If she had wanted to break Alcide's leg or back, she could easily have done it. Instead, she let that hoof come up off the ground. Alcide looked carefully, and saw that the hoof was perfect. He let it go, and looked up to the barn, where Henri was watching him. Alcide understood at once that it had been a test. Henri waved to him, and he waved back. As Henri went back into the barn, and Bijou walked away, Alcide saw that Esme was standing off, and staring at him.

"What is the matter with you?" Alcide asked. Esme

pinned her ears back and snorted. Alcide took a step in her direction, and she spun and bolted as far as the paddock would allow. Alcide said, "You were fine with me earlier." He held up both hands, but the mare did not relax. He turned and walked toward the barn to see if Henri had any real work for him to do.

The first dinner was a rushed affair, he was very tired, and Alcide took most of it back to the loft in the barn. Not fancy, but he was grateful. The radishes, picked a month ago, were actually still good. The small root cellars on the farm were quite effective, and now that the seasons were turning cooler, it was even easier to preserve. Extremely thin slices made crunchiness less important anyway, and between two pieces of hearty bread, slathered with goat butter, it was delicious.

Alcide preferred the earthy taste of goat butter to any other. When he had the chance to cook himself, he preferred how it melted more quickly, and even though the difference in the taste was sometimes lost on the stove, using it to bake made everything better. It made him miss his wife, though.

The second dinner, however, was more formal. Alcide had washed his face and hands, and put on the cleanest clothing he had. He left his hat in the loft, and carefully descended the ladder.

Welcomed into the house as a guest would be felt very nice indeed, and after some small talk with Henri, they all sat to eat at the table.

Henri lowered his head, and quickly said, "*Bénis-nous, ô Seigneur, et bénis ces dons que nous allons recevoir de Votre bonté par le Christ notre Seigneur, Amen.*"

Alcide was a bit caught off-guard by his use of "vous." He hadn't heard it in decades; he wondered if perhaps his relationship with God had become too informal. Henri looked up with a smile, and said, "It smells wonderful."

"I hope it tastes good," Seraphine said, grinning.

Alcide said, "I didn't see any ducks on the farm." He loved cuisse de canard confit, it was perhaps his favorite food, and it looked perfectly done on his plate. He wondered at the work she must have done, and in her condition.

"You have seen them now," Henri said, and laughed.

Seraphine also laughed, and shushed him.

Alcide took his first bite, and it was delicious. "Will you get more?"

Both Seraphine and Henri dropped their smiles, and Henri said, "Perhaps when I return."

Everyone took another bite of food. They each had two small potatoes, fondants. Alcide was still chewing some when he said, "Fantastic."

Seraphine grinned again, and said, "Well, any dinner seems a wonder after a mere radish sandwich the night before."

"There was nothing 'mere' about that," Alcide said

with a slight smile and a nod.

Seraphine nodded back, and looked at Henri, who said, "My wife is a wonderful cook."

"If you don't mind, please tell us of a wonderful city restaurant," Seraphine said. "I would love to go to a restaurant in the big city someday, maybe even Paris."

Henri said, "I'm sure it would be no better than this."

Alcide said, "I know that is true, and I'm afraid I don't have anything to say about the fanciest restaurants, but there was a lovely bistro not far from the apartment. They would serve quail eggs on salad, with vinaigrette and whatever fruit they could have fresh. Most often berries of some kind."

Seraphine said, "Simple."

Henri said, "But delicious, I bet."

Alcide nodded, and took another bite.

"Make it with frisée and lardons, it would be Lyonnaise. With warm vinaigrette," Seraphine said.

"Perhaps we should open a restaurant instead?" Henri said, smiling.

"I'm afraid that would take the fun out of it. I would be stuck in the kitchen, and without this fine company," Seraphine said.

Alcide lifted his head, a bit confused for a moment, and then said, "Ah, thank you."

"Do you have family around here?" Seraphine asked.

Alcide took another bite, chewed, swallowed, and then said, "None."

There was a bit of an awkward pause, and then Henri asked, "Can you imagine that Seraphine was one of five children, was the only girl, and was the baby?"

Alcide said, "You must have been the safest girl."

Seraphine laughed, and said, "I was! Perhaps too protected at times."

"I can imagine," Alcide said.

Seraphine looked at Henri, who smiled and then said, "They couldn't keep you safe from me."

"Maybe I didn't want to be safe from you," she said.

Alcide said nothing, and took a bite of his potato.

"Sorry, Alcide, if we embarrass you," Henri said, holding Seraphine's hand on the table.

"No at all. You seem very happy, as you should be," Alcide said, and then continued chewing.

They both smiled, and nodded.

Alcide then suddenly asked, "Do you eat the goats?"

There was a pause, and then Seraphine said, "Rarely. They really are here for the milk, cream, butter, and sometimes cheese. But, in the hardest part of the winter, if there is a goat no longer milking, then maybe."

"We don't butcher much here. I'm afraid most meals are eggs, or no meat at all," Henri said.

"This is an extravagant meal, then. I'm honored, and grateful," Alcide said.

"You're welcome," Seraphine said.

"And eggs are wonderful. So versatile," Alcide said.

"Certainly," Henri said.

"Neighbors will buy some, usually as they pass. Some milk, too," Seraphine said.

"You could formalize that, take a cart into town, and sell what extra there is," Alcide said.

"I have. It does work," Henri said.

"Perhaps we will do it more after you come home," Seraphine said.

"A nice idea," Henri said.

Alcide was willing to take a cart into town right away, Bijou could pull it, she being so even-tempered, but he sensed he should let the topic go for now.

They all finished eating, the men watching Seraphine eat the last of her food, save one bite. She leaned back, rubbed her round belly, and said, "I am full."

"You don't have room for a single bite?" Henri asked.

"Not in here," she said.

Henri reached over, grabbed the bite of duck with his fingers, and popped it in his mouth.

"Manners!" Seraphine said.

"I'm sure Alcide has seen much worse," Henri said, and grinned.

Alcide said, "I've *done* much worse."

Both Seraphine and Henri laughed, and Henri said, "I haven't heard you joke before."

"I wasn't joking," Alcide said.

Henri and Seraphine laughed again.

"I hope you had enough to eat," Seraphine said.

"I did, thank you, I feel like I might sleep for days

now," Alcide said.

"Would you like more milk?" Henri asked.

"Thank you, no," Alcide said.

Henri said, "You said you had done some carpentry."

"I have," Alcide said.

"And worked as a farrier," Henri said.

"Both," Alcide said.

"I was wondering about adding a loafing shed for the horses, on the far side of the meadow," Henri said.

"I see," Alcide said.

"Could you help me build one?"

"I could," Alcide said.

"Great!" Henri said.

"But we shouldn't," Alcide said.

"What? Why not?" Henri asked.

"Because you only have two horses," Alcide said.

"See?" Seraphine asked.

"And the land is small enough that the horses can come back into the barn for shelter any time," Alcide said.

"But there will be a third horse soon," Henri said.

"That foal will want to be with its mare much of the time," Alcide said.

"When would it make sense to add a run-in?" Seraphine said.

"You have four good stalls already inside the barn. I would think a run-in might be nice when you get your sixth horse," Alcide said.

"But we'll likely never have that many," Henri said.

"Well then, problem solved," Alcide said.

"Henri just likes to add on, and to build things," Seraphine said, with a smile.

"I'm ambitious," Henri said.

"That's fine. I just don't think you need it yet, and you asked. Of course, if you would like me to build something for you, I certainly will," Alcide said.

"We'll wait until we need it," Seraphine said, and Henri looked disappointed.

"I should go make a check on the animals, and get some sleep soon. The morning comes before the sunrise on some days," Alcide said.

"I'll go with you," Henri said, and both men stood.

"Thank you, Madame. It was a fine dinner," Alcide said.

"You are welcome, Monsieur," Seraphine said, with a slight bow.

Alcide bowed his head, and then both men went outside.

As they walked to the barn, Henri said, "I want to thank you, Alcide, for agreeing to stay here."

"You pay me, after all. A place and food now, and some money to come," Alcide said.

"It makes me no less grateful to know you are here," Henri said, and both men stopped walking.

"Of course," Alcide said.

"I trust you to take care of the farm, and of Seraphine.

My family," Henri said.

Alcide opened his mouth to speak, twice, but then only said, "I'll go to the goats first."

"Fine," Henri said, and clapped the older man on the back.

3
◇◇◇◇◇

THE CAVE
1914

East of the farm, where the forest floor rose at nearly a forty-five-degree angle, and the elevation approached 500 meters, there was a small, dry cave. The opening was as high as it was wide, but a man could not have walked in without ducking. It was partially hidden in the bushes, and those surrounded by pines. In the gap that allowed entry into the cave, half of the cleared space contained a small circle of stones, with charred remnants of wood in the middle.

Inside, the ceiling of the cave was a bit higher than the opening. Olivier sat there, on a pile of evergreen branches that he had dragged in. He was close enough to the mouth of the cave to have light, and far enough to be completely dry when it rained. The floor of the cave sloped down to the opening, so the cool air poured out, while any warmth rising up the face of the ridge came in. Sometimes, when it got quite cold, he built a fire outside the cave, in the circle of stones. He had tried it inside once, but the air was fouled for days afterwards.

He did his best to avoid having a fire, though, because it might be seen. He didn't want to be chased out of his cave, even by someone who thought they were doing a good thing. Olivier didn't want someone deciding what was best for him.

For cooking, he kept the fires very small. What he ate often did not require a fire, such as cheese, or a piece of bread. When he cooked, it was often just something on a stick, but he did have one small, charred, and dented pot. In this, he would boil eggs when he had them, or turn a root vegetable into a soup. A single potato, cut into small bits, would make a soup he would eat for a couple days. This combined with something like a frog, roasted over the coals, was all he needed. Olivier had long thought that large, festive meals came at much too high a social cost, with bowls filled with disappointment and derision. Also, the potential public depravation, as a punishment while others ate, was more power than Olivier was willing to ever grant anyone again. It was better to eat alone, he believed, food that you had gathered for yourself, even if some of it was stolen.

When Olivier was too cold to sleep, and it happened for a few nights each winter, he made a slightly larger fire. Olivier would warm himself through, with his back to the valley, hoping to screen some of the light. He would heat a number of round stones, right in the fire, as the wood burned down to coals. He then pushed a couple of these stones into the cave, near his sleeping spot, and left a couple out in the flameless glow, just in case. It wasn't a lot, and was perhaps more psychological than physical, but it helped.

He had a worn, wool blanket to cover him, and an old saddle pad that he put under his head. Even after all these years, he could still smell the horse it had protected from the saddle.

It was neither cold nor warm on this day. With a sharp pocket knife, Olivier whittled a piece of wood with care. It was soft, and about as thick as his wrist. Shaping it, he revealed from the wood the gentle curve of a back. Olivier smoothed it with his thumb, with the oil of his skin polishing it a bit, and then he began shaping it again.

She suddenly appeared in the mouth of his cave, and startled him. Olivier said, "You. What do you want here?"

She didn't make a sound, and instead simply stared.

"Don't you ever talk about this cave. You haven't, have you?" Olivier said.

She said nothing, and only stared.

"Did you bring any food?" Olivier asked.

She said nothing, but began shifting her weight slowly, back and forth from one foot to the other. Olivier reached for his water jug, and took a sip. "Want some?" he offered.

There was no response. Olivier shrugged and said, "Suit yourself."

He began whittling again. Then, without warning, while still standing in the mouth of the cave, she screamed a bloodcurdling cry. Olivier jumped and looked back her way, just in time to see her run off.

"What is wrong with you?" he shouted. He sat with his heart pounding, with a surge in his entire body.

Going back to his whittling, he spoke to the piece of wood in his hands, and said, "Crazy. A man would never shriek into a hole like that, for no reason at all. Why would she do that? Was she angry, or trying to frighten me? Maybe not crazy."

Olivier continued cutting away, perhaps with more force now. To himself, he said, "Witches. Women have magic. Some are kind. Very kind, some of them. Some are angry, some go mad. She's not mad, no, not mad."

He looked back at the mouth of the cave. "She's not mad. She's… stuck. Yes, stuck. Trapped. Frustrated. *Bloquée, bloquée. L'est prisonnière d'son esprit. Mais, mais, cependant, c'est une sorcière. Franchement.* Trapped, with magic."

Olivier began whittling again, and then imitated her scream, but barely audibly. And then he did it again. He looked toward the opening again, and put his whittling down. He walked over to a large, flat rock, and opened the folded scarf on top of it. Picking up a half-eaten loaf of bread, he examined it, and then plucked off a moldy corner. He bit off a mouthful from the remaining loaf, and rewrapped it, keeping the moldy bit in his hand. He walked to the mouth of the cave, and threw the green piece of bread as hard as he could into the trees.

Standing there, chewing, he scanned to see if she were hiding behind a nearby tree. Sometimes, he'd spot her watching the cave, but not this time. He imitated her scream again, but this time as a whisper, with a bread crumb falling from his mouth. He looked back at the scarf, and said, "I guess I have to work some more. Maybe eggs. Milk? Maybe cheese? I haven't had cheese in a long time."

He looked out into the forest again. A goldfinch, his crown of thorns visible, landed on a branch, and watched him. Another joined it, and then another. Soon, there were a dozen in the tree.

"Good to have company. When it's birds, and not witches," Olivier said.

The birds, in unison, took flight and disappeared into the forest. Olivier watched them go, sighed, and returned to the evergreen branches. He had another sip of water, and picked up his whittling again. He scored the wood where the belly would take shape, exaggerating the roundness, and then did the same for where the withers transitioned into a long neck. Olivier began to remove material, but not especially carefully, not yet. Revealing the crude, before the fine.

He heard running footsteps outside, and he dropped

his work to rush to the cave opening. Olivier scanned one way, and then the other. "It must be her again," he said softly, but he couldn't see her. He didn't want to call out, because if it wasn't her, he would be revealing his cave to another person. Olivier wasn't sure how she had found it in the first place. Whenever he came back here, he was careful not to be followed. Arsenault had tried to follow him once, but the farmer moved like an elephant in the woods, and Olivier had heard him. He had been able to lose him before they got halfway to the cave.

However, the girl was a different matter. "She probably followed me as a vapor, or as a crow," he said, under his breath. Whoever had come dashing by this time had made footfall sounds, with quick, short strides, but Olivier couldn't see anyone.

A bald, old man had come by once, with a dog, and the animal knew Olivier was there, lifting its head once, stopping, and looking right at him. The old man never took notice, and sent the dog farther ahead.

"I'll go tomorrow to the farm," he said to himself. "Maybe get some cheese. I wonder if he's gone to the war already."

Olivier went back to the evergreen branches, looked at the piece of wood, and picked up the knife. He wiped the blade on the blanket, and put it away. He lay back, staring at the ceiling of the cave, with his fingers interlocked behind his head.

"Everything will be different, and nobody can see

what it will be like. When someone leaves, it changes everything. When someone new arrives, it changes everything. Different words. Each person brings their own words. And energy," he whispered. Then, he mock-screamed again, with just a bit of voice in it.

4

◇◇◇◇◇

PARIS
1922

I asked Alcide, "So, no one knew where the boy, Olivier, was living? Did you eventually find out?"

"Be patient, I will tell you the story. But, no, no one knew at the time where the boy was staying, and what he was doing when he wasn't at the farm. He would disappear. I assumed then that he lived with people in a small house, where they didn't have enough food," Alcide said.

"But he wasn't?" I asked.

Alcide leaned forward, elbows on his knees, and said, "He was not."

"How did Olivier first start coming to the Arsenault farm?" I asked.

"They never told me," he said.

"He just appeared, from nowhere, one day and began working there?" I asked.

"I'm not sure," Alcide said.

"Is he really important to the story?"

"I will tell it, and then you can decide," Alcide said.

Staring at Alcide for a moment, I sensed he did not want to talk about Olivier yet, so I nudged him a bit by asking, "So, what happened next?"

"Next? I suppose what happened next was that Henri Arsenault left for the war. The neighbor, Claire, and her daughter Suzanne came to wish him well, and Father Benoit was there," Alcide said.

I asked, "Benoit was the priest's first name?"

Alcide exhaled loudly, and said, "His name was Father Benoit Albert."

"I see," I said, and scribbled notes. The old man's tone was especially effective at making me feel foolish.

"The priest laid his hand on Henri's head, and blessed him, and they prayed for his safe return someday soon," Alcide said.

"They prayed. Did Claire and Suzanne pray as well?" I asked.

"The girl bowed her head," Alcide said.

"And did you pray?" I asked.

Alcide paused for a moment, and then said, "Claire had her camera, and she was taking photographs."

"Of Henri and Seraphine," I said.

"Actually, I believe they were photos of local wildlife," Alcide said.

"What, really?" I asked.

"No," Alcide said flatly.

"Ah, I see," I said, with a grim smile. Made a fool of again, I decided then that I'd ask as few questions as possible during this interview. However, as I was to find out, that would prove much more challenging than I thought.

"She had her camera, and was intent on getting a photo worthy of the moment," Alcide said.

"And just in case," I said.

Alcide cocked his head, nodded, and said, "Just in case he would not return. Perhaps that is what we are doing with every photograph we take. Putting ourselves permanently in a place and in a time. They are expensive, after all."

"Quite expensive. I suppose people will never take photographs for granted, and will always be selective," I said.

Alcide asked, "Are we capturing others? Or grand vistas? Or is it that we are creating proof that we, the photographers, were there?"

"If that were the case, we'd probably find some way to put ourselves in the photographs we take," I said.

Alcide sniffed, and said, "I suppose we'll never be that self-important."

"I hope not," I said.

"In any event, she had her camera, and said she was trying to provide photos for the separating wife and husband," Alcide said.

5

◇◇◇◇◇

MONTAGNAT
1914

Henri had not been issued a uniform yet, as he had not yet reported for service. On the day he left, he was in civilian clothing and, wherever he went on the farm, Seraphine was clasping some piece of it. She clung to his sleeve, or gripped a handful of his shirt at his abdomen. He stepped away, and she grabbed his belt at the small of his back, from which he then towed her.

Each time Claire aimed the camera at them, Henri and Seraphine froze, with granite smiles and devastated eyes. Once the photo was taken, Alcide could almost see them shrink, as if their bones softened each time.

Eventually, Father Benoit called everyone to come closer. Holding both hands up in front of him, his palms facing Henri and Seraphine, he said, "Our Lord, we pray that You take this young couple into Your heart, and to safeguard young Henri as he goes to protect what is just, from what is evil. We pray that You watch over this small farm, and all those who are on it, and to comfort Seraphine during the difficult wait for her husband's return. We pray for their unborn child, until he or she can be baptized into Your grace. Grant them all peace and courage, Lord, in these trying times, until we can all return to this same place, and praise Your holy name. Amen."

The priest then laid his hand on Henri's forehead, and whispered an additional prayer. Henri's eyes closed, as did Seraphine's. Alcide could not hear the words clearly, but thought the priest was likely speaking in Latin. Some languages change the look of the speaker's face. When the prayer ended, Father Benoit stepped away, and forced a smile.

"Seraphine, step over here," Claire said.

"Take pictures of Henri," Seraphine said.

"This one is for Henri. I'll give it to you, and you can send it to him," Claire said.

Alcide watched, as Seraphine tried to smile, and she brushed hair from her face. Just as Claire appeared ready to take the photo, however, Seraphine said, "Wait, not with the barn in the background."

"Why not? It's a nice barn," Claire said.

"We're too close to it. It will just be a wall. Here," Seraphine said. Moving to her left, she stood with the paddock behind her.

"Fine, that is lovely," Claire said, looking through the lens. The camera clicked as she took a photo, and then, just as she took another photo, the mare Esme charged into the frame and nearly collided with the fence. She whinnied loudly, and Seraphine turned to look, and there was a third click.

"Ah, I think that last photograph was wasted," Claire said.

"What is it, Esme?" Seraphine called.

The mare bolted away, and then charged back. Henri and the priest walked that way, and everyone else followed, except for Suzanne. Alcide glanced back at the girl, who was standing perfectly still, hands at her sides, staring at the ground, with her hair draping around her face. Esme snorted, and Alcide turned to see the horse spin and gallop away.

Alcide was last to arrive at the fence. He placed his forearms on the top rail, and watched Esme trot in a wide circle.

"A snake?" Father Benoit asked.

"I've never seen her behave that way because of a snake," Seraphine said.

Esme slowed, and came to a halt, but with head up, and ears back. Bijou, the other mare, slowly walked toward her.

Claire said, "Bijou will calm her."

Suddenly, just as Bijou arrived at Esme's side, a loud "*towooo*," came from above the paddock. Standing just outside the fence was the enormous plane tree and, in its branches, a large tawny owl called again, "*towooo*."

Esme half-reared at the sound, and Bijou leapt away from her. Behind them all, Suzanne screamed.

"Oh, sweetie!" Claire said, and rushed toward her daughter.

Esme again charged the fence where the rest of them were standing, and everyone stepped back except Seraphine.

The owl called once more. Alcide said, "That's not a good sign."

The priest said, "Please, don't start with your Cagot superstitions."

Suzanne, held by her mother, shrieked again. Esme galloped away and out of sight, around the corner of the barn. The owl sounded again, Suzanne screamed again, and still unseen around the corner, Esme whinnied.

"Does this seem normal to you?" Alcide said to the priest.

The owl took flight on silent, serrated feathers, and was soon gone. Suzanne was in her mother's arms, and Seraphine was soon in Henri's.

"You shouldn't go now. Not after all that. You heard what Alcide said," Seraphine said to Henri.

The priest stared at Alcide.

"You know I have no choice," Henri said.

Claire called, "I will take Suzanne home. Henri, keep safe, and come home soon." She walked away, still holding her daughter as they walked.

"I'm so afraid," Seraphine said.

"I will be home again before you have time to miss me," Henri said.

Father Benoit said to Alcide, "You see what you did? Raising her anxiety, and in her condition."

"Father, it's alright. Leave him alone," Henri said, still holding Seraphine.

"Henri, have tea with me, to settle our nerves, before you have to leave," Seraphine said, but then they heard the truck approaching.

"I will get your bag," Alcide said.

"Can't you leave tomorrow, on another truck? There must be another. All of France cannot move to the war on a single truck," Seraphine said.

Alcide walked toward the house, and as he passed where Suzanne had been standing and screaming, he noticed a small puddle on the ground. He shook his head, went just inside the door, and retrieved the bag. He returned with this to Henri, just as the truck came to a stop.

Seraphine had her arms around Henri's shoulders, weeping, and he kissed her head. Henri reached for the bag, and Alcide handed it to him.

"*Allons-y*, Arsenault," a man from the truck called.

Seraphine and Henri released each other, the priest raised a hand in one more blessing, and Alcide nodded. Seraphine turned as if to embrace the priest, but then turned and fell against Alcide, who held her just enough to keep her upright.

"I love you, Seraphine," Henri said, and he walked toward the truck.

Seraphine openly weeping still, said, "I love you, too. Come back to us."

"I promise," Henri said. He threw his bag up to another man in the back of the truck, and had not fully climbed in before the truck began to move.

"Take care of things, Alcide," Henri called.

Alcide raised an arm straight in the air, and then let it drop as the truck drove out of sight. Father Benoit took Seraphine from Alcide, and guided her into the house. Alcide was left alone, and he looked toward the horses, who stood side by side, heads and ears high, and who seemed to have watched the entire scene play out. Esme seemed no more disturbed than Bijou was. Alcide looked up to the branch where the owl had been perched. *Midday*, he thought, *an owl calling in midday. Not a good sign.*

Father Benoit came back outside, and seemed to read Alcide's mind.

"They sometimes hunt in daytime," he said, "You should not have said what you did, about it being a bad sign, on the very day her husband is leaving for war. It was insensitive of you."

"In your prayers, you said that he was going to fight against evil. He is going to fight against men who came from farms just like this, with their own priests praying just what you did," Alcide said.

"They are invaders," the priest said.

"Invading because of an alliance they have, just as France has thrown in to this madness due to an alliance France has with another, who threw in because of another alliance. It is a war of promises," Alcide said.

"Of honor," Father Benoit said.

Alcide looked across the way at Esme, who was still watching, and then he scanned the horizon the owl had flown towards. "I expect blessings from you, and perhaps even giving comfort in hard times, but I cannot look to the Church for lessons in honor," Alcide said.

"Because priests are blessing enemy soldiers, too?" Father Benoit asked.

"Because my people can still see the side doors on churches, churches that we skilled few built for you. Short doors, built for us, to shame us, to make us stoop as we entered while everyone else walked into church with heads high," Alcide said.

"Come now, that was long ago," Father Benoit said.

"Priests would carefully administer the Holy Eucharist to others, and then throw the bread at us in our pews, as if we were filthy dogs. How we scrambled to catch it midair, to protect the sanctity of it. How blessed we felt to even consume it," Alcide said.

"Not all priests did that," the priest said.

"The kind ones used long-handled wooden spoons," Alcide said.

"This does not mean the Church, and the people

who believe, are all without honor," Father Benoit said.

Alcide lowered his voice, took a step closer, and said, "A wealthy man, one of the few of my people who had scratched out a place for himself, dared to step into a church and dip his hand into the font meant for the 'clean' people. He was caught, called 'Cagot,' and those honorable people chopped off his hand, and nailed it to the church door as a warning."

Father Benoit was silent.

"So, don't talk to me about honor," Alcide said.

Father Benoit went back to the topic of the war, and asked, "So, it's not honorable to defend one's land?"

"If someone tries to take what is yours, completely unprovoked, then it is clean to defend oneself. But shedding the blood of those your government has labelled as your enemy is not as simple, and declaring again and again that it is honorable does not make it so," Alcide said.

"But they are trying to take our land!"

"We declared them our enemy before they invaded. We sided with Russia, who sided with Serbia," Alcide said.

The priest was clearly angry, and asked, "Where did someone like you learn of all this? Where did you learn of France's alliance with Russia, and of these other alliances?"

"Someone like me? What do you know of me except that I am Cagot, *des gens des Marais*? What more do you know than that in my old age, I choose to work as a farmhand, to help these poor young people, who are at the mercy of governments and churches, and promises they themselves did not make?" Alcide said.

Father Benoit said, "This way of thinking explains the fate of your unsophisticated people. *Sine doctrina vita quasi mortis imago.*"

Alcide replied, "Our fate? *Astra inclinant, sed non obligant.*"

Father Benoit stepped back, looking surprised, with his jaw working. "She was right. She suspected you are educated. Why are you hiding here? Are you a criminal?"

"I am not," Alcide said. "I am here to work."

"But why this work? If you know some Latin, you had at least some classical education," Father Benoit said.

"Most of the Apostles were laborers, fishermen, and the like. There is nothing wrong with sweat," Alcide said.

"One was a tax collector," Father Benoit said.

"Matthew, yes," Alcide said.

The priest's eyes narrowed, and he said, "Surely you were not admitted to seminary?"

"I'm just a simple farmhand," Alcide said.

The priest stared a moment longer, before turning and walking away. Alcide watched him go for a minute, and then headed for the barn. In the distance, beyond the paddock and the trees, he spotted some movement. He shielded his eyes and, between the trunks, he recognized that it was Olivier, running parallel to the tree line, and then disappearing into the woods.

6

◇◇◇◇◇

PARIS
1922

"Why was Olivier running? What was he doing in the woods? Had he heard what you and the priest had said?" I asked Alcide.

"Honestly, I doubt he overheard. He was quite far. I suspect he watched us say goodbye to Henri, and then as the priest and I spoke," Alcide said, but then shrugged. "Perhaps he caught some of what was said."

"How odd. Did he often appear at the fringes like that?" I asked.

"He did what he did. It may seem odd, but people are how they are. I know what it is to be an outsider. To be on the fringe, as you say, and looking inward," Alcide said.

"But it's different for a lone boy. You were in a culture, and within your own people, your own community," I said.

"A community pushed and held out on the edge. We were mocked, derided, and attacked. There was no path to earning a place in polite society," Alcide said.

"And yet, you just mentioned a man from your community, who had become wealthy. The man whose hand was cut off. How did he accumulate wealth if you were all blocked out?" I asked.

"His mother was one of us, but his father wasn't. He looked more Irish than Cagot, and his earlobes were long. He left our part of the village while still young, and set out. He returned educated, with money, and began to help us," Alcide said.

"He helped your people how? Did he bring money?"

Alcide said, "He brought hope. I wasn't a little boy anymore, but he found a teacher who would come to us. A young one, who had been dismissed from the lycée for political reasons. I learned to read, and then could also teach myself. You have no idea what that meant to us. It opened up the world," Alcide said.

I made a couple notes, and then decided to press. "Did you attend seminary? How much education did you ultimately attain?" I asked.

His shoulders fell a bit. "Not enough to escape feeling like I was a stranger to my own land. When they took his hand and nailed it to the door, I had returned to the village only the night before. It was then that I stopped my studies, because I knew it would never change anything," Alcide said.

"You had left, in order to study? Where had you gone?" I asked.

"Not far enough," Alcide said.

"What does that mean?" I asked.

"And in some ways, too far. Once you leave your group, when you return to them, even to those same people, you become an outsider yourself. You can neither return to the familiarity of the group of outcasts to which you once belonged, nor can you blend into the larger group that cast your people out. It is social limbo. The Fields of Asphodel," he said.

"The fields of what?" I asked.

"Never mind."

Pausing a moment to reflect, I then asked, "So, was Olivier an outcast among outcasts?"

"Even among our small group, on the island the farm had become, Olivier was different. We did not push him away, nor degrade him. In fact, she was kind to him, as if she hoped he would warm to her. It was someone else who had rejected him. Someone much more important to the boy had shunned him long before, and that really shaped him, so Olivier lived in a world of his own construction. He had built for himself his own reality; it was one he could fully comprehend. We saw Olivier only when he needed to get food and the like," Alcide said.

"He wasn't living with other people?" I asked.

"He lived alone," Alcide said.

I shifted in my seat and said, "How awful."

Alcide smiled, looked at the floor, but then looked me directly in the eyes, and asked, "Have you ever tried it?"

"I haven't. I would expect it would be terribly lonely," I said.

"As people have long said, there is a difference between being alone and being lonely," Alcide said.

"Well, they are certainly connected. How can one be alone and not lonely?" I asked. Leaning forward, I said, "You obviously cannot be lonely with many people around you."

Through stiff lips, Alcide said, "Actually, that can be the worst sort of loneliness."

7

◇◇◇◇◇

MONTAGNAT
1914

In the time before Seraphine first heard from Henri, Alcide stayed very busy, doing more than he had expected, because they had not seen much of Olivier. Seraphine, for her part, was becoming less concerned with all of the animals, and this was especially noticeable with Esme. It seemed to Alcide that their mutual condition had not brought woman and horse closer. In fact, the bond they had once shared seemed to be loosening.

From the handpump, Alcide splashed cold water on his face, and then was headed for the goat pen when he spotted Olivier walking his way, coming from the tree line, and rounding the corner of the paddock. Just as Alcide inhaled to say something to the boy, Seraphine stepped out onto the porch.

"Olivier, you're back," she said. "I am glad to see you are well."

Alcide watched as the boy looked down at her swollen abdomen, but then he lifted his gaze, removed his hat, and asked, "Would it be possible to work for some cheese today?"

Seraphine looked to Alcide, and asked, "Do we have cheese to spare?"

Alcide looked at Olivier, and said, "We do. Also, there are still root vegetables, in the second cellar."

"Give us a hard day's work, and take potatoes and cheese with you," she said to Olivier, but she didn't wait for any acknowledgment before turning and going back into the house.

Olivier put his hat back on, and asked, "Has she been sad?"

Alcide said, "Her husband left."

"So of course she would be sad. I was here that day, you know. Over there," Olivier said, pointing towards the trees.

"You know, I saw you. Why didn't you come and wish him well? You have known them much longer than I have," Alcide said.

"What matter is that of yours?" Olivier asked.

Alcide stared at the boy for a moment, before heading to the goats. He said, "Check the horses. Bijou is messy at her back end. Clean her up, and give Esme a good brushing, but keep in mind the state she is in. She may kick or bite."

The boy said nothing, and headed for the horses.

Alcide fed the goats. He pulled one doe called Fern up onto the wooden milk stand that he had rebuilt, secured her neck between the bars, and placed a container of feed beneath her head so she could continue eating. He washed both teats, and then worked the teats to let the first of the milk fall away uncaught. The first of it would spoil the rest, he believed. Only then did Alcide place the pail beneath her, and began milking.

Alcide heard Bijou nicker, but then nothing else from her. Birds landed nearby, and pecked at the ground, while unseen birds sang. He whistled while milking, an old medieval tune called *Belle qui tiens ma vie*, and then chuckled a bit at himself. Pulling the bucket away from Fern, Alcide quickly washed the teats again. Then, he patted her back, and set her free from the milkstand.

He took the pail in through the nearest door, poured the milk through a screen and into a glass jar, capped it, and placed it into the nearby icebox, beside the cheese that Olivier had asked about. Ice was lasting longer now, as the days grew shorter and colder. Alcide cleaned up, and then went to find the boy.

Stepping into the larger part of the barn, below the loft where Alcide slept, he spotted Olivier standing beside the mare, Esme, who was on crossties, and huge with the foal she was expecting. In Olivier's hand was a brush, thick with horsehair that had been pulled from the animal, but he was no longer brushing her. His wrist was over her withers, not moving, and Olivier was caressing the horse's shoulder with his face. His eyes were closed, and he had a weak smile on his face, but it was the first time Alcide had ever seen Olivier smile. He silently rubbed his cheek, again and again, on the animal.

Alcide looked at the barn floor and took a step, scuffing it on purpose to make noise, and took another couple steps, and looked up. Olivier was still working the horse's side, but with the brush this time.

Just then, a woman's voiced called from the barndoor. "Is there anyone there? Seraphine?"

"Who is that?" Olivier asked.

"Lucille Dubois. Madame Dubois is the midwife. How is it I could know, but you do not?" Alcide asked.

"Not for Esme?" Olivier asked.

"Idiot. *You* are the midwife for Esme," Alcide said, pointing.

"Hello?" Lucille called again, and then appeared.

"Madame Dubois, she is in the house," Alcide said.

"Oh, thank you," she said, as she stepped into view. "You're out here alone, then? I thought I heard talking."

"I'm right here," Olivier said.

She squinted toward the boy and the mare, and said, "Oh, so you are. I'm afraid I don't see well in the shadows. I knew a man had been hired, but I didn't know a boy as well."

Olivier gestured toward her, while looking at Alcide, as if to say, "See? She doesn't know me either," but he said nothing aloud.

"He's been helping here for some time before I arrived," Alcide said.

"Oh?" she said.

"For a long time," Olivier said.

Alcide wondered exactly how long it had to be for a boy to call it a long time.

"How nice, then. Not so much for you to do then," she said, looking at Alcide.

Alcide looked at the floor, and said nothing.

"Well, I'll go to the house then," Lucille said.

"Would you like me to take you?" Alcide asked.

"I've been there many times, I'm sure I'll manage, but thank you just the same," she said, and then turned and carefully picked her way back. Looking down, looking forward, looking down, looking forward, and then stepping out the door. Alcide thought she walked like a pigeon.

"A blind midwife?" Olivier asked.

"Be quiet. She'll hear you," Alcide said. "And she isn't blind."

Alcide heard her making her way to the house, yelling, "Seraphine? Seraphine, are you home?" He winced.

"She cannot even see a house," Olivier said.

"Finish what you are doing with that animal, and then tend the chickens. I assume you have already cleaned up the other horse," Alcide said.

"She was a mess. How long has she been like that?" Olivier asked.

"It started a couple days after he left for the army, and we moved the horses to the smaller pasture," Alcide said. "But we moved them back yesterday. The horses were tearing up grass."

"Pulling up the roots while grazing," Olivier said.

"How did you know?" Alcide asked.

"The soil beneath the grass in that field is very sandy. Bijou got that way because she was pawing the grass up with the roots, and eating all of it, sand included. She shouldn't graze there," Olivier said.

Alcide said, "Esme was grazing the same pasture."

"Her teeth are better. She cuts the grass off, and eats only the grass. Bijou can't do that," Olivier said.

Alcide thought this was very insightful of the boy. "Where did you learn this?"

"We once had a fifteen year old gelding who did this. He had no front teeth at all," Olivier said.

"Well, we can't put one in one pasture, and keep the other in another. The horses will never stand for it," Alcide said.

"That pasture cannot be used then," Olivier said. "But I'm not sure about the horses being upset. Bijou is avoiding Esme now, and Esme does not pursue her either. I tried bringing them closer together, but they were not interested."

Alcide paused, narrowed his eyes a moment, and then relaxed. "Tend the chickens next."

Olivier pulled the brush down Esme's side once more, without saying anything.

Alcide began to turn away, but then asked, "What ever happened to the gelding with no front teeth?"

Olivier stopped brushing, shrugged his shoulders, and said, "I don't know."

Alcide wanted to ask more, but didn't. Returning to the goats, he saw one of them stumble, and then again. He called out, "Olivier!"

As Alcide reached the unsteady goat, Olivier appeared. "Look at this one," Alcide said.

"What is it?"

"Clumsy," Alcide said, and then waved his hand in front of the goat's eyes. The animal had little response.

"Can't see?" Olivier asked.

"Not well. We switched them over, but this one has had too much grain, and not enough forage," Alcide said.

"So, no more grain, but what else can we do?" Olivier asked.

"Hold the goat," Alcide said, and then strode back into the barn. Going to a shelf, he scanned a few bottles, and found the one he wanted. He returned to Olivier and the goat.

"What is it?" Olivier asked.

"The animal has polio," Alcide said.

Olivier immediately released the goat.

"You can't get sick from goat polio. You didn't have goats on that other farm? Let's get this into her," Alcide said.

Olivier hugged the goat's neck, and Alcide lifted its chin.

"Medicine?" Olivier asked.

"Thiamine. Once she gets a taste, it won't be hard to get her to take it. Goats love the taste of it," Alcide said. He poured some into the goat's mouth, and even after it swallowed, it licked its lips repeatedly.

"What does it taste like?" Olivier asked.

Alcide offered the bottle.

"No, I won't," Olivier said.

"No more grain for this one. When she eats, just roughage," Alcide said.

"For how long?" Olivier asked.

"She needs thiamine a few times a day, and for quite a while, even after she seems better. Only forage at first, and add grain in slowly over the next few weeks," Alcide said.

"It's getting impossible to find green forage," Olivier said, looking around.

"It is, and we have to avoid beet greens, turnip, kale. We have to keep the sulfur down, or it will work against us," Alcide said.

Olivier nodded, and then asked, "Should we give some thiameed to the midwife?"

Alcide said, "Thiamine. Tend to the chickens," and off Olivier went, without another word.

The midwife, Lucille, was suddenly in the door, and said, "Excuse me."

Alcide startled and turned.

"Oh, I am very sorry," she said.

"Is there something I can do?" Alcide asked.

"Well, since there is no man of the house, I'm not sure who else to tell. I suppose I could tell Claire Voisine. Yes, I suppose I will," Lucille said.

"Tell what? Is the baby alright?"

"A bit quiet, but yes, I should think so. It is Seraphine. She is doing all the usual things. Creating a space for the baby; it's warm and inviting. But she seems so melancholy, which I know is to be expected, with her husband gone off to war," Lucille said.

"And we've heard nothing," Alcide said.

"Not one letter?"

"Not yet," Alcide said.

She took a step closer and said, "I know it's not your place, and it is not why you are here. You have much to do. But I can come by only once per week, until it is time, so I wonder if you couldn't spend more time with her. As company. Just so she isn't alone."

"But she's not alone. I'm here, and Olivier is here," Alcide said.

"She is alone in that house. She is without conversation, or company of any kind," Lucille said. "It's not good for her to be alone so much."

Alcide looked toward he house and said, "You're right."

"Good," she said.

"You're right that it is not my place, and it's not why I'm here," Alcide said, and her smile fell.

"Ah, but, you could be of comfort. You need not attempt to be entertaining, or even interesting. You can just be yourself," she said.

Alcide looked at her.

"That is not what I meant," Lucille said.

"I know what you meant," Alcide said.

Lucille paused, and then said, "Good." She turned, and carefully watched her own feet as she found her way out of the barn again.

8

◇◇◇◇◇

MONTAGNAT
1914

He felt anxious as he knocked on the door. When Seraphine opened it, she smiled, and asked, "Yes, Alcide?"

Pulling his hat off, he said, "Good day. I thought I would check to see if you need anything. I know it gets more difficult, in your condition, to... well, to do anything. I am able to help in the house as well, Madame, if I could make things easier," Alcide said, but then felt a wave of nerves. It felt odd to ask to be let in, even if only to help, and with a woman young enough to be his granddaughter. Alcide had lived through a great deal in his life, but these simple things still affected him. Partly because of his ethnicity, and partly because, despite everything, he was still a decent man.

Seraphine smiled more broadly, and said, "That's very kind of you," but suddenly her face fell, and she looked past Alcide.

"What is he doing?" she asked.

Alcide looked back, and saw Olivier with Esme in the paddock. The boy was standing beside her, rubbing his cheek on the horse, sort of hugging her.

"He's become very fond of her. I saw him doing this while the mare was on crossties also," Alcide said.

"How bizarre," she said, but then she looked at Alcide once more, and invited him in.

"So, what can I do?" Alcide asked.

She was rubbing her rounded belly, which now protruded well beyond her full breasts. Seraphine said, "Would you mind bringing in more wood for me, Alcide?"

They walked to the back of the house, and Seraphine stopped just short of the door, but Alcide stepped out, pulled on his hat, and went to the sheltered woodpile. He filled his arms, returned to the house, and went to the wood crib beside the stove. It had once been an open fireplace, but now a wood stove sat on the grey stone hearth, and the metal stove pipe disappeared up the chimney, behind a hand-carved stone mantle.

He carefully stacked the wood in the crib, and went out for more. It took six armloads to fill the crib, which had been nearly empty. When he was a younger man, it might have taken only four trips, because he could carry a larger load in those days. Still, he was in decent shape for a man his age. The loads were smaller, but he was not winded.

Alcide removed his hat again, and went to find Seraphine. The midwife had said to offer her company and, while he was grateful for the chore he could do for her, he would try a bit more conversation.

"Ah, there you are," she said, startling him.

He said, "The wood is in. Is there anything else?"

"Would you like some tea, or coffee?" she offered.

Alcide was surprised, and grateful, that the visit had turned a bit social on its own.

"Maybe a glass of water?" he said.

Walking into the kitchen, she said, "Of course. Please sit." She motioned to the table.

Alcide sat, and lay his hat in his lap. Seraphine returned with two glasses of water, placed these on the table, and after making a quick turn, placed a few biscuits as well. She sat, a bit clumsily, across from Alcide. They each took a sip, and she lifted a biscuit.

"How are things going, Alcide? Are you warm enough in the barn? The nights are turning cool," she said.

Alcide's mind jumped to sleeping in the house, he blushed a bit at the thought, and said, "I am quite comfortable at night, thank you. The blankets and the hay are just fine."

Seraphine sat back, held her belly, and hummed.

"Uncomfortable," Alcide said.

"I can't seem to find a good way to be," she said.

Alcide nodded, knowingly.

She leaned toward him, as much as she could, and

asked, "Have you ever married? Any children?"

He just looked at her. It was a normal question to ask, but it was one he had not answered in a long time.

"I'm sorry. A personal question. I apologize," she said.

"I was married, and we had a little girl," he said.

"I'm sorry. I shouldn't have," Seraphine aid.

"We lived in Paris, where we had met. We had been students together. I was working at the newspaper, *La France*, and we were happy," Alcide said.

"What was your little girl's name?" Seraphine asked.

"Viola," Alcide said.

"How beautiful," she said.

Alcide paused, and looked at the biscuits.

"This seems painful for you," Seraphine said, "Please, don't feel obliged…"

"The newspaper ran many stories about the coming war with Prussia, but it seemed so unlikely. So far away. But it wasn't," he said.

Seraphine put both hands on the table, but then removed them. She said, "War always seems far away, until the last moment, when it's in your life."

"My daughter was three years old when they surrounded and laid siege to Paris. At first, it felt like we could hold out forever," Alcide said.

"They shelled the city, didn't they?" Seraphine asked.

"They did not want to capture a leveled Paris, it seemed, so at first, they attempted to starve us," Alcide said.

"I have heard of this," she said.

"The people of Paris grew skinny. Every animal at the zoo was consumed by the desperate population," Alcide said.

"My Lord," she said.

"Butchers in their shops became experts at cleaving dogs and cats into meat, but even those poor creatures were struggling to find food," he said.

Seraphine put her hand out on the table, palm side up, as if offering to hold Alcide's hand, but he did not take it. He cleared his throat, and there was a rumble of thunder outside.

He said, "Sounds like a storm coming."

"Your family succumbed to the hunger, then?" she asked, looking out the window.

"After a time, the Germans did begin shelling Paris. I guess they decided they had waited long enough. Ultimately, they fired more than 10,000 shells into the city, but they killed very few people," Alcide said.

"Thank God," she said.

He stiffened. "I was out, looking for food. My wife, and my child, were among the few that were killed by the shelling. I came home to find the face of our apartment building had collapsed after being struck by German fire. I found my wife's body, broken, and in the street."

"Oh no! And your daughter?" Seraphine asked.

"Viola was never found. Sometimes, I dream that she survived, taken in by a kind family, and raised with love," Alcide said.

"Let's hope so," she said, and her eyes were wet.

"More likely, she…" Alcide began, but was interrupted by a knock at the door. It was the neighbor, Claire, and she let herself in.

"Seraphine?" she called.

"I'm in the kitchen," Seraphine said, wiping her face. Alcide stood, and so did she.

"If there is anything else I can do," Alcide said, as Claire entered the kitchen carrying her camera and photographs.

"Thank you," Seraphine said, placing her hand on his upper arm.

"Oh, hello," Claire said with a smile.

"Good day, Madame," Alcide said, bowing his head slightly.

"Is it raining?" Seraphine asked Claire.

"Not yet, but the sky is dark, and there is lightning. I thought I might be caught in it on the walk here," Claire said. She held up the camera, and said, "I thought we could take pictures of how pregnant you are, for you and Henri. And I have these."

As Claire spread the photos on the table, Alcide could see they were of the day Henri left.

"Oh, I miss him so much," Seraphine said, touching the one closest to her. There was another clap of thunder, louder this time.

"I better get to the animals," Alcide said, and yet more thunder. He left the house and walked quickly into the barn. There he found Esme and Bijou in their stalls, with Olivier adding hay to the hanging wall feeder for Bijou.

"Well done. It sounds like quite a storm," Alcide said, although not even he heard the end of his sentence over the next thunder. Both horses had their ears back, and Esme began stomping her front, left hoof.

"That's odd," Alcide said.

"They are never bothered by storms," Olivier said.

There was another clap of thunder, this one sounding as if it were right above the barn, and both horses backed up in their stalls—kicking, snorting, farting, and whinnying.

"Esme, Esme, it's okay," Olivier said, moving toward her. Esme's eyes were wild, as the boy began to open the stall. Alcide stepped quickly, pulled Olivier back, and pulled the stall door closed just in time. Esme rushed forward and struck the door.

"She wouldn't hurt me!" Olivier said.

A crack and boom of intense thunder just then, and Alcide said, "She very nearly did."

Seraphine and Claire came rushing into the barn. The horses were besides themselves, screaming in between thunder claps.

"What is the matter?" Seraphine asked.

"Are they always like this?" Claire said.

Bijou kicked her stall so hard, Alcide was not sure how much more it could take.

"Never," Seraphine said.

"We don't know. Maybe because the storm is so intense?" Alcide said.

Olivier was reaching into the stall, trying to reach Esme, when she reared and struck at his hand with both front hooves, and missed.

"Come away from there!" Seraphine said.

"Back up, boy," Alcide said, pulling on his arm, Olivier came back with them.

The next sounding of thunder was less intense, as the storm began to move off. Both horses were still very upset, but settling slowly.

"I just don't understand it," Seraphine said.

"There was certainly something different," Alcide said.

Olivier stared into Esme's stall, and said nothing. Alcide decided he'd have to watch out for Olivier more closely. The boy was very nearly hurt.

"What was it?" Seraphine asked.

"I do not know. Perhaps they fed off each other's energy. As one got more riled, it panicked the other, and so on back and forth," Alcide said.

"Like I said, they are not close friends like they used to be. Maybe they had some sort of disagreement," Olivier said.

Claire said, "You talk about the animals as if they are people. As if they had a heated debate over some topic."

"Maybe they did. Just not with words, like we do," Olivier said.

"Horses are remarkably smart and sensitive. Maybe there is tension between them, and the storm brought it out of them," Alcide said.

"How can we know that? How can something like that be proven?" Claire asked.

"I am willing to take it on faith. Besides, it would be much more frightening if we *could* prove it," Seraphine said.

9

◇◇◇◇◇

MONTAGNAT
1914

A letter from Henri

When Seraphine received her first letter from Henri, it was mid-September, and ten days after he left. Alcide was just coming out of the barn when he spotted her walking from the road, the letter already open, and she was reading as she walked.

Looking up from it, she said, "A letter from Henri!" and grinned.

Alcide was glad for the boost in her spirits, and didn't expect to hear any of the contents of the letter, until she suddenly began reading it aloud.

"I arrived safely. We were issued our uniforms and equipment, and we have begun our transformation into soldiers. We are still in training, and so are not yet prepared to join our comrades already in the fight. We have been assured that there will be plenty of war left for us, although I would be perfectly fine if it were not so. While I am proud to be here, as every true Frenchman is, how I already miss you and the farm," she read, and tilted her head. She took a breath and continued reading.

"We have heard that our armies and our allies are making a stand, a defense of Paris, and that the Germans have gotten quite close to the city," Seraphine read, but then she stopped and looked at Alcide.

"It is alright," Alcide said.

"An enemy approaching Paris, though. It must bring up memories. I'm sorry I read that aloud without looking ahead," Seraphine said.

"Quite alright," Alcide said. "Read more if you like."

She looked down, read a bit silently, and then aloud said, "There are men here from all over France. Many of them are farmers, so I am left wondering who will feed this army, and France. Although, I am sure, that you are managing fine."

Alcide said nothing.

She continued reading, "From when I was a boy, I have many fond memories of my own father, my mother, Alma, and I all going for a picnic."

"Alma?" Alcide asked.

"His sister. She lives near La Rochelle. We rarely see her," Seraphine said, and then, "My mother would spread food on a blanket. There was nothing fancy, but we loved to sit in the sun and eat the hardboiled eggs, apples, and pieces of bread she had packed."

Alcide said, "Sounds lovely."

"I miss those days, and I know soon we will have days like that with our own family. Sun on our faces, eating and laughing. Maybe with strawberries! Please be sure to write to me, and tell me all that is happening there with you. I am told that when the baby comes, if I am still in training, or if I am assigned to a unit which is not actively engaged, I may be able to come home for a day. I do hope so," she read. Seraphine smiled, read ahead silently again, and then said, "It becomes a bit more personal. I think it best to stop there."

Alcide nodded.

"It is so good to hear from him," she said.

"I'll get back to work," Alcide said.

"Have a nice afternoon," she said, and turned for the house, while still reading to herself.

Alcide thought of Paris, and of an enemy at the city's gates once more. He wondered how many times in history that had happened before, and if there would be any future wars to imperil the capital.

A vision of his daughter's face filled his mind. Alcide wondered if there were three year old girls in Paris, perhaps about to be surrounded once more by Germans. If Viola were still alive, she would be a middle-aged woman. Alcide thought that if life had been fair, he would perhaps have a room in her house, and have dinners with Viola and her husband, and that she could take care of him as his body fell apart over the coming decade. Her children would visit to listen to his stories.

Instead, Alcide kept his stories mostly to himself, with no one with whom to share, although he had told more lately.

Alcide knew he didn't have another twenty years to collect stories, because he'd been hard on his body, and he had already lived more years than his relatives normally had.

As he walked toward the barn, he looked back over his shoulder at the house, and saw Seraphine enter he house.

He said, "There may be more stories yet."

10

◇◇◇◇◇

PARIS
1922

Alcide rose, and I did, too.

"Sit, Robert," Alcide said, and I complied. The old man walked to the railing, and looked out over the roofs. I inhaled to ask if he was alright, and before I could, he held up one hand. Waiting, I wasn't sure if I should even exhale.

He said, "It was the next night, with yet another storm, that Seraphine and the mare, Esme, both went into labor. I went to fetch the priest and the blind midwife."

I said, "I thought you said she wasn't blind."

Alcide turned, faced me, and leaned back on the railing. "If I ask you not to speak for a little while, and to hold your questions so that I can tell this part of the story, would that be unreasonable of me? Do you think it is something you could manage?" Alcide asked.

His tone was different, and not sharp. Instead, it

was earnest, and I felt no desire to push back. I simply nodded, and made some notes.

Alcide took a deep breath, and said, "I will tell you everything, and I will trust that your honor as a man will guide you when you decide what should be published and what should not. I no longer trust myself to decide what is proper, or even normal. The envelope of acceptability has been stretched over the years for me, and I no longer care enough about what others think to be able to judge what to withhold from you. So, I need you to do that for me, and for her. For Henri, for Olivier, and the others. Can you?"

"I will do my best," I said.

"Very well," he said, "I left and collected the priest and the midwife, and upon returning to the farm, I could hear Seraphine crying out from inside the house. The midwife and priest rushed that way, and I headed for the barn, where I found Olivier trying to comfort the distressed mare, Esme. In the next flash of lightning, I could see both the horse and the boy were nervous."

11

◇◇◇◇◇

MONTAGNAT
1914

Alcide was in the barn, when he heard Olivier call for him. Walking over to Esme and the boy, Alcide looked beneath the mare.

"Her milk is dripping," Olivier said.

"It's the first sign. She is going to foal tonight," Alcide said, and there was a distant clap of thunder. Esme did not seem to react to it, as she and Bijou had during the last storm.

Olivier held a lantern; it was getting just dark enough to need it. Alcide said, "Hang that before you drop it in this straw." Olivier did as he was told, and hung the lantern on the post where it belonged.

"This is her first, so I think it will be a while yet," Alcide said.

Olivier licked his lips, and said nothing. Esme seemed only a bit anxious, and was still eating out of the hay bag.

The muscles in her shoulders twitched, and every now and then, she held her tail up for a few seconds.

Nodding back in the direction of the house, Alcide asked, "Does she know about the foal coming?"

Olivier shrugged, and said, "I didn't tell her, so I suppose not."

Manure fell from Esme into the straw, and Olivier said, "That's the second time already."

"That will happen throughout. We won't walk her around too much. This straw is clean, and when she goes down, we don't want her in that," Alcide said.

"Should I tie her then?" Olivier asked.

"Leave her free to move in this space. I only mean we won't encourage her to spread that all over," Alcide said.

Olivier nodded, and said to Esme, "Everything will be alright," and patted the horse gently by the withers.

"I should go tell her," Alcide said.

"I'll stay here," Olivier said.

"I won't be long," Alcide said. He walked out of the barn, and to the door of the house. While knocking, he removed his hat. When the door opened, Seraphine was standing there, obviously in pain, and holding her own abdomen. Alcide stepped quickly inside and helped her to a chair. Lowering her into it, he said, "Do you want me to get help?"

"Get Madame Dubois, bring her here, please. Please, go quickly. Oh, and Father Benoit. Please, Alcide, hurry," she said.

"Stay in this chair. Don't try to go anywhere else. I will be right back," he said.

"Wait! Why did you knock? How did you know?" Seraphine asked.

"I didn't. I came to tell you that Esme is in the same state. I'll get them," Alcide said.

He moved quickly out of the house, and to the barn. From the door he shouted, "Olivier!" There was a clap of thunder.

"What is it?" Olivier asked from inside the barn.

"I am going to get the priest and the midwife. Stay with the mare. I won't be long," Alcide said.

"The baby is coming tonight, too?" Olivier asked.

"Yes, both the foal and the baby, but stay with the horse. Do you understand?" Alcide said.

"I will," Olivier said.

Alcide knew that Olivier would have been of no use to Seraphine, and probably would have only caused her more stress and anxiety. He also knew that Olivier wanted to be with Esme.

Within thirty minutes, Alcide returned with Father Benoit and Lucille Dubois. No sooner had they arrived than those two ran into the house, the priest guiding the midwife. Alcide walked quickly to the barn, and entered just as the rain began to fall. The next flash lit every crack in the barn walls, and a peal of thunder rattled the rafters above.

"Boy?" Alcide called.

"We are here!" Olivier said, a then he added, "Some red liquid was just dripping out of her."

"Really? That seems a bit fast," Alcide said.

"Will she be okay?" Olivier asked.

"Haven't you done this before?" Alcide said.

"I've been there when it happened, but it was never this important to me. I never really paid attention," Olivier said, "Is the foal coming right now?"

"I think it will be hours yet. How has she been with the thunder?" Alcide said.

Olivier exhaled loudly, leaned against the fence, and said, "This time, it doesn't seem to bother her."

"This could be a very long night," Alcide said.

There was more thunder.

"Have you checked on the other animals?" Alcide asked.

Olivier shook his head.

Alcide said, "The other horse is only a few stalls away, and you didn't even check on Bijou?"

"I've stayed right here with Esme," Olivier said.

There was another flash, and before the next thunder clap, they both heard the woman, Seraphine, cry out.

"How can we hear that?" Olivier asked.

"They must have the window open for fresh air," Alcide said, looking in the direction of the house.

"Should you go look?" Olivier asked.

Alcide shook his head. "She has all the help she needs. I'll tend to the other animals."

Olivier said, "I did make sure the chickens are away and locked tight."

"Good. I'll start with Bijou," Alcide said. She was fine, but a bit anxious. She seemed a bit more agitated than Esme. Leaving the barn, he glanced over and saw the chickens were, indeed, locked safe in the coup. He turned the corner, and walked through the gate for the goat pen. All the goats had moved inside their small barn, enclosed on three sides, with the floor covered in straw. They were all set to ride out the storm.

Lightning flashed again, and then came the thunder. The rain had not really increased in intensity. When Alcide returned to the barn, he found Olivier sitting on the fence, and Esme had a sheen of sweat on her neck and haunches. She lifted her head in what appeared to be a silent whinny, and then lowered it.

"It hurts, doesn't it?" Olivier asked.

"It does," Alcide said, and put his hand on her back.

"Why should it have to hurt? To have a baby?" Olivier asked.

Alcide said, "I will surely multiply your pain in childbearing. In pain, you shall bring forth children."

"What does that mean?" Olivier asked.

"God. The pain is meant to punish women, because of Eve's sin. All women are in pain when giving birth," Alcide said, looking at his feet.

"But the animals, like Esme... animals don't sin," Olivier said, but then added, "Right?"

Alcide looked at the boy and said, "Animals commit only one sin, but it has grave consequences."

"What is it?" Olivier said.

Alcide looked up into the rafters, and said, "They trust us."

Olivier looked at Esme, jumped down from the fence, and stroked her long nose. He said, "Don't trust us, Esme. Not even me. And your sin will be forgiven."

Alcide looked at Olivier, and wanted to offer that without souls, animals could not be held accountable, but he stayed quiet. They both heard Seraphine cry out, again, from the house.

"Will you stay here with us the whole time?" Olivier asked.

"We can take turns sleeping in the loft if we get tired. One of us will be with her all night, and I promise that when the foal comes, we will both be here," Alcide said.

There was more thunder and lightning, and Olivier said, "This storm is lasting a long time."

"It is still raining, but not as much as you would think," Alcide said, and he sat on a bale of hay. Olivier looked at Alcide for a moment, and then sat on a nearby bale. Neither spoke for some time. Esme turned now and then; she was all sweaty, and even more milk was dripping.

"Why would the horses ignore thunder in the past, be so upset at it in the last storm, but not now?" Alcide asked.

"Maybe it wasn't just the storm," Olivier said.

"What does that mean?" Alcide asked.

"Some people say that lightning is a weirding sort of light. That the flashes reveal what we can't see in normal light," Olivier said.

"So, you are saying the horses could see in the lightning flashes that which we could not see?"

"Maybe," Olivier said.

"Like spirits?" Alcide asked. "Do you believe in such things?"

"Of course, don't you?" Olivier asked.

At Seraphine's next cry, Olivier said, "Should you go check?"

"I'll stay here," Alcide said.

Olivier looked relieved, but he looked in the direction of the house again. Neither spoke again for quite some time. There were more flashes, the sound of thunder, and the cries from the house. Esme was silent until about another hour had passed. She munched a bit of hay, with her tail held high, and then a bit of yellow fluid fell from her. Olivier was on his feet immediately, but, in a soft voice, Alcide said, "Easy, don't spook her now."

"Did you see that?" Olivier asked.

No sooner had he asked it than a larger amount of the same fluid fell from her again.

"There!" Olivier said.

"I know," Alcide said.

Seraphine screamed from the house.

Esme then seemed to slowly lower herself to the straw, and before she was down, the yellow fluid gushed out of her in great quantities.

"That's normal?" Olivier asked.

"I thought you said you've seen this before," Alcide said.

"So, she's okay. This is supposed to happen," Olivier asked.

She's fine," Alcide said, just before the thunder sounded again.

A large yellow bag of fluid then partially emerged, slack and wet, translucent.

"The foal is deformed!" said Olivier.

"Be still. Get back on the bale," Alcide said.

"Are you sure?" Olivier asked.

"That's only the bag of waters. The foal is inside of it," Alcide said.

Alcide watched Olivier return to his bale, and then looked at Esme, who was lying a bit off-center, but not down flat on her side. The horse was looking back at what was happening. Esme looked like she might try to stand back up, but then a hoof appeared within the sac, and then more of the fluid drained into the straw bedding. Esme's eyes were wide, as she slowly swung her neck back to look, and then away, and then back to look again. The horse was silent, and you could see her straining to work the foal out of her body. She slowly lay over flat on her right side, and another huge amount of fluid came out of her, spraying out around the foal, and down into the straw. The sac fell limp around the hoof.

"The foal can't breathe in there," Olivier said.

"Be calm. She'll work this out," Alcide said.

Esme rolled up enough to lift her head to look back once more. A bit of straw came up with her head and hung from her right ear. Both of her ears turned toward the house when Seraphine screamed again.

Olivier said, "I wish she would have that baby already. Her wailing is making this worse."

"I'm sure she's looking forward to it, too," Alcide said.

Olivier said something more but it was drowned out by the thunder, and Alcide never heard what he said. Suddenly, Esme did stand up, and both of the foal's front hooves came through the sac, and stuck out of Esme, into midair, dripping. She turned, and ate a bit more hay, the hooves still protruding, with no additional progress.

"Do we have to pull the foal out?" Olivier asked.

"It may come to that, but not yet. Give Esme more time," Alcide said.

Esme turned her body 180 degrees, stood facing them, and then lowered her head to eat some more. Olivier craned his head, as if trying to see the foal's progress, but neither of them could see around the mare. After more time had passed, she turned away, and Alcide could see the foal had made no progress. Olivier inhaled, but before he could say anything, Esme went down again, this time immediately lying flat on her left side.

"Is she alright?" Olivier asked.

Alcide said nothing.

Seraphine's next scream from the house was overlapped by the next thunder clap.

Next, with great heaves, and with her right, rear leg held in the air, the foal began to inch its way out. Esme rolled up, as if she may attempt to stand again, but immediately lay back down.

Seraphine screamed, and then the midwife's voice came, "Wait! Stop!"

At the next clap of thunder, Esme's whole body began heaving again.

"I see the face!" Olivier said.

Alcide saw it, too. The foal's nose, mouth, and eyes were already out, but covered in sac. Esme's breathing was loud, as she rested momentarily. Esme half-rolled again, and then was back down again.

Thunder rattled the barn itself, and when the echo began to fade, Seraphine cried out once more.

Esme was quiet except for the heavy snorts. Prey animals, such as horses, had evolved to be silent in their most vulnerable moments. Esme stood again, but exhausted, with a foal's nose and two front hooves sticking out of her, she stumbled, caught herself, and then lay down once more.

The midwife's voice came again from the house, "Seraphine!" followed by Seraphine's scream of pain. Alcide remembered his daughter, Viola, being born. The labor had lasted more than ten hours, but everything had gone well, with a doctor and a nurse present in their apartment. He had waited, as fathers did, in the next room with a couple of friends from work. There had been screaming, but only at the very end. Seraphine had been crying out, as if in agony, for several hours.

Thunder sounded again, and a large flash of lightning. Alcide was amazed, too, that a September storm had maintained such ferocity, and for so long. He looked at Olivier. The boy's hair was matted to his head with sweat, even though the air was cool, and his face was contorted with worry.

Esme began pushing again. The foal's entire head came clear with each push, and then slipped back in to the ears.

"The foal has a blaze!" Olivier said.

With a few more pushes, the foal's shoulders came out. The little front hooves, and the nostrils were free of the grey-white sac. The rest of the foal and sac quickly followed, except for its rear hooves, which remained inside Esme. With a shake of its head, the foal was clear of the sac back to its ears. It began working its way forward in the straw, trying with only its front hooves, to crawl out of the sac which had held it for so long. Esme was no longer pushing, she only lifted her head and looked back, watching. As she watched, Esme began instinctively licking the air, as if inviting the foal to come and be cleaned.

"I can't wait any longer. Let's just pull the rear hooves free," Olivier said.

"Leave them alone. Just watch. The worst is over. We only need to watch the foal eventually get up and find a teat," Alcide said.

Seraphine let out such a cry from the house that it made Alcide jump. He was, at this point, much more concerned about the woman and baby, than the mare and foal. Finally, the foal came free, of both its mother and the sac. It dragged itself closer to her head, but Esme didn't stand. She licked the foal, and the foal nuzzled her side, looking for its first meal. She continued to lick him, and soon, the foal was trying to stand. Suddenly, Bijou whinnied loudly, and then again. Esme didn't make a sound, as the foal got three of its four hooves beneath it.

Then, they could hear Seraphine groaning loudly. Alcide stood before the foal did, and said, "Don't do anything to speed it up, but watch closely to make sure he nurses from her as soon as they're standing. Don't try to help. Do you understand? Only watch."

"I will," Olivier said. Bijou whinnied again.

"I am going to the house to check. I'll be right back. Don't interfere with those horses," Alcide said.

"I won't," Olivier said.

Alcide turned and headed for the house. Once the foal got that first feeding, there would no cause to worry, he thought. As he crossed from the barn to the house, there was a flash, followed almost immediately by its thunder.

He thought he saw something in the field, and then he heard screaming, but it wasn't Seraphine. He shielded his eyes from the raindrops, and waited for the next flash. When it came, he saw her. Suzanne, the neighbor girl, was out in the field, arms stretched upward, soaked in her white nightshirt, screaming at the sky.

"Good Lord," Alcide said.

Suzanne screamed again, and then Seraphine groaned again. Just as another flash illuminated Suzanne for a second time, the priest came out of the house onto the porch, and then thunder shook the ground. Suzanne suddenly was silent. Alcide scanned the dark, but couldn't see, and when he next flash came, Suzanne was gone.

Alcide approached the priest, and asked, "How is she?"

Father Benoit said, "The baby, a girl, was stillborn."

"Oh no. And Seraphine?" Alcide asked.

"The bleeding stopped, but she is in some shock. She will not speak," Father Benoit said.

Seraphine's groan came again.

Alcide looked past the priest, but Father Benoit said, "It would be better if you left her to the midwife."

He knew what it was to lose a child, and while Seraphine had never held her living baby in her arms, he knew that her loss was unimaginable to those who had never suffered it themselves. Alcide asked, "How will Henri be informed?"

"I will notify my contact, in the chaplain service, and they will get word to Henri," the priest said.

"I see," Alcide said, "A damned shame, really."

"Ah well, how's the mare, and the foal?" the priest asked.

"What?" Alcide asked.

"The mare. Did that go well?" the priest asked.

Alcide blinked at the man, looked past him at the house once more, and asked, "Did you baptize the child at least?"

Father Benoit said, "The Church does not permit the baptism of a stillborn child."

"Why not?" Alcide asked.

"How can we say this baby will have a lifelong commitment to the Gospels?" the priest asked.

"And the child's soul?" Alcide asked, "I assume the Church is still concerned about our souls?"

"We trust the infant's soul to the mercy of God, even though she stopped attending Mass after Henri left. Seemed like especially poor timing to me, but that is not really for me to decide. I remind you that the great mercy of God wants the soul of all men to be saved," Father Benoit said.

"And little girls, too," Alcide said.

"Of course," the priest said.

"Can the baby get a proper funeral?" Alcide asked.

"I will conduct the rite of committal, likely the day after tomorrow," the priest said.

"Where is the baby now?" Alcide asked.

"I am not sure. Probably wrapped in blankets, in a bassinet," Father Benoit said, paused, and then asked again, "How is the horse?"

Alcide turned and returned to the barn without answering. The priest had watched as a woman's heart and soul had been shattered minutes before, there had been a child born without life in her, and he was asking about a farm animal. Father Benoit did not follow Alcide, and it was just as well.

Entering the barn, he found Olivier had kept his word, and was once more up on the fence, smiling, watching as mare and foal stood beside each other, with the wobbly youngster nursing hungrily.

Alcide's eyes met Olivier's, and the boy asked, "What's wrong?"

"The baby is dead," Alcide said.

Olivier looked at the floor, and asked, "And, how is she?"

"Alive, but I didn't see her. The midwife is tending to her," Alcide said.

He watched Olivier, who seemed frozen for a moment, until the boy said, "I was in here, so happy, smiling, while that was happening in there."

Alcide said, "You could not have known."

Olivier stared at the ground, and was slowly shaking his head. "How can joy exist so close to heartbreak? You would think that they would collide in the air between,"

Olivier said. Lightning flashed, and thunder sounded.

Alcide said nothing, walked over, and put a hand on Olivier's shoulder. The boy slowly shrugged it off. Neither of them said anything more. They only watched the foal nurse.

12

◇◇◇◇◇

PARIS
1922

Alcide looked at me and said, "Two days later, we buried that baby on the farm. Not on consecrated ground, but instead on a small knoll in the field."

"Because the baby had not been baptized," I said.

"Can you imagine the ego it takes to make decisions like that? To deny that baby a place in a cemetery? The man claims to believe in all of it with all his heart, preaches humility, and then has the gall to... surrendering that baby's soul to the mercy of God. If God is so merciful, He would instruct His church to baptize the stillborn and to lay them to rest on holy ground," Alcide said.

There was nothing to say to this. I could see the pain in Alcide's face.

He looked away, and said, "It did seem properly done, at the grave, I mean. Claire Voisine did most of the crying as she stood beside Seraphine, with one arm around her. Seraphine didn't make a sound, her lips were sealed, but she did shed tears. She didn't look at the casket much, nor the priest, nor any of us. She mostly looked off toward the trees."

I took a few notes, and asked, "Why do you say it was 'properly done?' Did you think it might not be?"

Alcide did not reply directly, but instead said, "I remember the priest read from Isiah… 'On this mountain, He will destroy the veil that veils all peoples, the web that is woven over all nations; He will destroy death forever. The Lord God will wipe away the tears from all faces.'"

"Seems a proper choice," I said.

"And a couple lines from Revelation, which began with… 'Jesus Christ is the firstborn from the dead…'" he said.

I said, "That's a bit odder."

Alcide said, "But I think the trouble to come in this story—and I will tell you about it—may have begun, I mean, where a seed may have been planted, was when Father Benoit read from the Gospel of John, to include… 'When Jesus saw his mother and the disciple whom He loved, He said to His mother, 'Woman, behold, your son.' Then He said to the disciple, 'Behold, your mother.'"

"Can you tell me now about the trouble to come?" I asked.

Alcide seemed to ignore my question, and said, "It was only when we lowered that little casket into the Earth that Seraphine made a sound. She said only, 'Where have you gone? Where are you, little one?' She said this softly, again and again, until Claire gently guided her back toward the house. They all departed then, except for the priest, Olivier, and me. With the casket lowered, the boy and I filled the grave with the soil taken from it, and then marked the grave with a small wooden cross I had fashioned. The priest stood and watched. Once we were finished, the priest said only, 'So very sad,' as he turned and walked away."

"It is a sad story," I said, and jotted some more notes.

"Later that day, Esme was nursing her foal in the paddock. The little filly was called Elise. Ironically, it was Olivier who came up with the name, I think. Anyway, as I was walking between the paddock and the house, I caught sight of Seraphine. She was inside the house, at the largest window, looking out toward the paddock. Standing there, alone, she watched that mare nurse her filly. Seraphine was clutching her own breasts, and although I could not really hear her, I could see that she was sobbing," Alcide said.

"How awful," I said.

"She then pulled at herself, as if she wanted to rip her breasts from her body, and she swayed with the sobs, like wheat in a storm," Alcide said.

His eyes were glazed in recollection. I was sure he was lost not only in that memory, but in his own remembered pain at the loss of his daughter. Not knowing what to say,

I pretended to make a note of something, not knowing what I might write either.

I thought of the profound effect grief has on the mind—a layering of love with pain, creating a terrible scaffolding which amplifies each. The enormous confusion at being faced with the incalculable loss of the person, and every future experience denied, along with the irretrievable portion of oneself the dead took with them. My own grief was, in no small part, why I had come to France... but that was another story.

"Robert?" Alcide asked.

I looked up, and he was staring at me. "I'm sorry, did you say something more?" I asked.

"I didn't, but you look a bit stricken," Alcide said.

"You painted quite a scene," I said.

"There is much more to come. Are you sure you are up for it?" he asked.

Taking a deep breath, I said, "I am."

13

◇◇◇◇◇

MONTAGNAT
1914

Claire came by to check on Seraphine. Alcide, coming out of the goat pen, had followed her as she went to the house. She climbed the steps, but he stayed off the porch. When Seraphine answered, Claire asked to be let in, but Seraphine blocked the door, and Alcide heard her say that she did not want company.

"But it's not good for you to be alone," Claire said.

"I am very alone. It's all I can be right now," Seraphine said.

"Come outside then and we can take a little walk. Even if we don't talk, you can get some air," Claire said.

"I don't want air," Seraphine said.

Claire said nothing for a moment before saying, "Seraphine, I am worried about you."

"Go tend to you daughter," Seraphine said, "And leave me to mine."

Claire's head fell, and without another word, Seraphine closed the door. Claire turned and left the porch, and stepped toward Alcide. She said, "She cannot simply hide in there forever."

"It is only the second day since the burial," Alcide said.

"But she's all alone," Claire said.

"By choice. You did a nice thing, to offer company, knowing what the visit would have been like if she had let you in. She didn't. She hasn't spoken but a couple words to me since the night she lost the baby," Alcide said.

Claire looked back toward the house, and asked, "Do you think she may harm herself?"

"I have no idea. If she has decided to, there is precious little any of us could do. She is, as she said, alone. However, I think she will find her way back," Alcide said.

"Do you really believe that?" Claire asked.

"Her behavior is just as one would expect, given the tragedy she is experiencing, and with her husband absent throughout this terrible time," Alcide said.

Claire tilted her head and asked, "You were not always simply a farmhand, were you?"

"A simple farmhand?"

"I meant nothing by it," Claire said, "I will come by every couple of days. Will you let me know how she is doing, even if she won't see me?"

Alcide nodded. "Although we have some out in the milkroom, I do have to enter the house for certain foods still. I may not learn much from her, but I can at least see her condition."

"I don't mean to suggest that you should spy on her. I am only worried about her, and I can't stay here," Claire said.

Alcide nodded again, but then asked, "Can I ask you something?"

Claire waited.

Alcide said, "The night of the storm, when Seraphine was in labor. I saw your daughter. I saw Suzanne."

"Go on?" Claire said.

"She was standing out in the field. The night was black, and there was rain, but in the flash of lightning, I could see her out there... I could hear her over the falling rain... arms stretched to the sky, screaming," Alcide said.

Claire said nothing.

"Why did she do that?" Alcide asked.

Claire took a breath, and then said, "Given the chance, she would do it in every storm. The more power in the storm, the more determined she is to get out."

"That was certainly a powerful storm that night," Alcide said.

"When a storm comes, I often will just hold her," Claire said.

"I understand," Alcide said.

Lowering her voice, Claire said, "With some storms, I have had to tie her to the chair to keep her in."

Alcide said nothing at first, but then asked, "But that night…?"

"I had no idea the storm that was coming. When she went for the door, I grabbed her. For the first time, ever in her life, she fought me. She thrashed and kicked, and even bit me," Claire said, lifting one sleeve just enough to show bruises that were clearly teeth marks.

"And that's how she got away," Alcide said.

"From me, yes, but I got to the door first, and locked it," Claire said.

"So…" Alcide began.

"That is when she hit me from behind with a pan," Claire said flatly.

Alcide's mouth fell open.

Claire straightened, and she said, "When my back was turned to her, while I was locking the door, she struck me with a pan. When I woke, the door was open, and the floor was wet with rain. The pan was lying beside me. I stood quickly, to go out into the dark after her, and my knees buckled. I went to the floor again, and when I woke again, Suzanne was with me. It was day, I was in my bed, and Suzanne was sitting on the edge of my bed. She was crying, rocking, and holding my hand."

"The girl got you to bed?" Alcide asked.

"Suzanne is remarkably strong," Claire said.

"And have you seen a doctor? You might have been killed," Alcide said.

"My head has hurt ever since, but the pain is diminishing each day. I'll be fine," Claire said.

"Has she ever attacked you before?" Alcide asked.

"She did not attack me! She panicked, as a bird would in a net. It was more my fault than hers, the way I tried to trap her in there," Claire said.

"This bird almost killed you," Alcide said, "What's wrong with her, anyway?"

"Not a thing. Just a wild spirit that keeps her from sitting long enough to learn the niceties. As her father says, 'There will be time enough for all that someday.'"

"Have you ever considered…?" Alcide began to ask.

"An asylum? Never. Others have suggested it, but just imagine. Look how she panicked to get out of her own home. Can you think of what being locked in an asylum would be like for her? She will never go to one of those places," Claire said

Alcide took a deep breath, and said, "I'm sorry. I pressed too far."

"Please just keep an eye out for poor Seraphine. I'll come back in a few days to check in," Claire said, but her tone had hardened.

"I will," Alcide said.

With a nod, Claire left. Alcide watched her go, and then looked over at the house. Turning, he went to tend to the chickens.

◇◇◇◇◇

Later that night, Alcide woke in the dark loft. Dawn was a long way off. He lay there, thinking about the baby out in the cold grave, and then he thought of Viola. If his daughter had a grave, he did not know where it was. He had searched for her, and with every overturned bit of debris from that Paris apartment, he had expected to find her, but never did. His wife's gravestone had two names on it, but only one of them was beneath it.

Alcide also thought about what Claire had said about her daughter, Suzanne, being a wild spirit. Of the three daughters—Seraphine's, Claire's, and his own—Suzanne was the one survivor. Alcide thought that maybe a wild spirit was necessary for a daughter to survive in this world, but at what cost?

He also wondered if Henri had been told yet of the loss of his baby. If so, had he received the news while standing in a field? Or perhaps called off the line, and told while sitting in a command post, or maybe in a church? Alcide suspected the news was probably brought to Henri, and given to him right where he stood.

Then, Alcide heard a sound. Outside, in the night, a noise not unlike a dove. He listened, and heard it again, and a mechanical squeaking. Alcide got up, and walked to the hay door. Looking down, he saw Seraphine was at the pump. Her back was to him, and she was nude from the waist up. She pumped again, the handle rising and falling, ice cold water rushing out of the spout onto her heavy breasts. Seraphine caught the water, and rubbed it into her skin. Alcide could see the water in the basin was cloudy with her milk. She rubbed her breasts a few moments longer than the water ran, and then she pumped more. As it splashed onto her again, she groaned, and Alcide knew that it was so cold as to be painful. Still, just as she had before, she worked to express her milk, into the frigid gush of water, and let it wash into the basin beneath.

He could not turn away at first, watching her try to wash her milk and pain away, but then as if breaking free from a spell, his head snapped away, and he felt a rush of guilt and pain. He returned to his bedding in the hay. Listening, he could hear the squeak of the pump handle, and then the gasp and groan at the water's coldness.

Alcide had no idea what to do. Should he speak to her? Bring her into the house, with his blanket around her shoulders? Then, there was no sound. No grief sounds, no squeaks, until he heard the door to the house open and close. Why had she come outside for that, he wondered? Why the coldest water? In the dark, she would not have been able to see as far as the baby's grave. Did she not want the warmth of the house while her child lay in the cold ground? Alcide lay back, and stared into the dark rafters. He understood what agony and grief were, but he couldn't fully understand why she had done that. He was a man, after all.

14

◇◇◇◇◇

MONTAGNAT
1914

Not long after sunrise, Olivier arrived, and Alcide found him with the mare and her foal. As Alcide approached, he saw the boy trying to lead and turn Esme, while Elise followed. Esme's ears were back, and she shook her head.

"Olivier, move away. You're upsetting her, and I think the filly wants to nurse," Alcide said.

"That is why I am doing this. She wasn't letting Elise eat," Olivier said.

"Move. Let me see," Alcide said.

Olivier stepped to the fence, and when he did, the filly attempted to nurse from Esme, but the mare turned away.

"See?" Olivier asked.

"Is this the first time you've see this?" Alcide asked.

"She always let her nurse before," Olivier said.

"Strange," Alcide said.

Elise tried again and again to nurse, and Esme seemed to only get more agitated. The filly became more insistent, and the movements of the horses became more intense. Olivier stepped forward to try to intervene.

"Olivier! Back up!" Alcide said, but Olivier did not, and Esme lashed out with a front hoof, grazing the boy's shin. He yelped and jumped back.

"Are you hurt?" Alcide asked.

"It stings, but nothing broken. She would never hurt me. What's wrong with her?" Olivier asked.

"I don't know," Alcide said.

"Will she hurt Elise? Will she hurt her own baby?" Olivier asked.

"Maybe. We could pull the foal away, and give the mare a rest," Alcide said.

However, before they could do anything, Esme turned on her foal, biting Elise on the neck and throwing her down.

"Oh no!" Olivier said, but before Alcide could say or do anything, Seraphine suddenly appeared, shrieking and running directly between Esme and Elise. Seraphine dropped and draped her body over the filly, screening her from Esme.

"Don't hurt her!" Seraphine said.

"Good Lord!" Alcide said, leaping forward, grabbing Esme's lead rope, wrenching it hard, and getting the mare's attention. Alcide pulled, leading Esme away from Seraphine and Elise beneath her, and the mare didn't fight him. Esme followed as Alcide led her outside to the paddock, and let her go. The line trailed on the ground beneath her as she trotted away.

Alcide went back and found Seraphine kneeling, with the filly Elise calmly standing beside her.

Olivier asked, "Is Esme okay?"

"She's in the paddock. Go get that line off her," Alcide said.

Olivier ran past him and out. Alcide looked at Seraphine, and asked, "Are you unhurt?"

"How could she do that?" Seraphine said, and stood, rubbing Elise's nose.

"I don't understand what has happened," Alcide said.

Seraphine turned to Elise, placed a hand on her withers, and said, "We'll take care of you."

"How are you? We haven't spoken much," Alcide said.

"I know. I'm not right," Seraphine said.

Alcide took a deep breath, and asked, "You don't want to hurt yourself?"

"I don't want. I don't think. And until I saw Esme hurt her own baby, I thought I could no longer feel," Seraphine said, as she stroked Elise's neck.

"If Esme has rejected her foal, we will have to come up with a plan. We could certainly use your help," Alcide said, hoping this would give Seraphine something to be involved in.

Seraphine asked, "How could she reject her baby?"

"It's very odd. Normally, they will reject a foal from birth, or else accept it. For her to allow Elise to nurse and then shun her is strange," Alcide said. "At least, the foal got that first milk." Then, he thought of Seraphine at the fountain, and then drove the image from his mind.

Olivier came back in, and said, "Maybe Esme is sick? Or injured?"

"We'll check her over. Get blankets on Esme and Elise. If they will be apart, we should try to keep them warmer," Alcide said.

"I'll sleep with Elise tonight," Seraphine said.

"You can't sleep out here," Alcide said.

"I could sleep with Esme," Olivier said.

"Esme will spend the night out," Alcide said.

"Why? She didn't really hurt the foal," Olivier said, "She only wanted to be left alone."

Alcide looked at Seraphine and asked, "What do you think?"

"I don't care. As long as she can't attack Elise again. You can put her anywhere you want," Seraphine said.

"We can put her in the stall closest to the cross ties. Maybe if she were tied there, she would let Elise nurse," Olivier said.

"It's a bad idea. Even on cross ties and hobbled, she could hurt the filly badly," Alcide said, "She might be more upset if tied and unable to walk away."

"Should we even try it?" Seraphine asked.

"It's difficult to bottle feed a newborn foal. It takes a lot of work, and nothing is better than her mother's milk," Alcide said.

"Can we put Esme's milk in a bottle?" Olivier said, but he didn't wait for an answer, and went outside.

"I've never heard of a mare tolerating it. It makes sense, but the horse has to be willing. They aren't like goats. They have a different temperament," Alcide said.

"So, what do we do?" Seraphine asked.

"If we can't get Esme to cooperate, we will start with goat milk," Alcide said.

"We can get cow milk if we need to," Seraphine said.

Olivier came back in with Esme, and led her to the farthest stall from Elise and Seraphine.

Alcide said, "Cow milk is not as good for horses as goat milk is. If we have to get cow milk, aside from having to get it, we'll have to add water, and some of that apple starch you use for making jams."

Seraphine said, "I see. It's that different?"

Alcide said, "Cow milk has too much fat, and not enough of the right sugars. Goat milk is closer to horse milk. With the goats you have, we will probably be okay with ten liters per day to start, but as Elise grows, we will need more."

Olivier asked, "For how long?"

"Months," Alcide said, "but we'll introduce soft, mushy grains earlier than normal. Also, I have seen once, long ago, a foal was taught to drink from a bucket. We can try it. It's a matter of training Elise to drink from it, and keeping the milk fresh."

"Seems so unfeeling. No contact, just raised by a

bucket. All the more reason for me to stay with her, at least while she is a baby," Seraphine said.

Alcide paused, and then said, "We can stick to the bottle. It is a lot of work, though, as I said."

Olivier asked, "What about Esme?"

"We can try again," Alcide said.

"I don't want that horse coming near Elise again. I don't trust her," Seraphine said.

"Maybe she is hurt or sick," Olivier said, patting Esme's shoulder.

Seraphine said to Alcide, "Keep her away from Elise. Something horrible can happen in an instant."

Alcide nodded.

"Will Esme be okay? What will happen to her milk?" Olivier asked.

Alcide looked at Seraphine, and could see that she was serious about not having Esme near Elise again. He said, "Walk her regularly. Her milk will dry up in four days, maybe five. A damn shame."

"I'll take care of Elise," Seraphine said.

"And I'll take care of Esme," Olivier said.

Alcide scratched his head, and walked away. One caring for the mother, and the other mothering a found baby. Alcide thought that no good could come of this.

15

◇◇◇◇◇

MONTAGNAT
1914

The chickens having been tended to, Alcide came into the barn, and found Seraphine with Elise. She had scarcely been anywhere else. Spending day and night with the filly, Seraphine wouldn't let anyone else care for her. Since the last bottle feeding had gone well, Alcide wasn't particularly worried—not about Elise anyway.

Olivier was fine with the arrangement, and was often with Esme a couple of stalls away, as he had been before the foaling. He had also gotten better about not neglecting Bijou and the other animals.

Seraphine was reading to Elise, and didn't know Alcide was there. She read aloud, "…and what picnics we three will have, near the stream."

Alcide cleared his throat to announce his presence.

She turned, and her voice cracked a bit when she said, "I received a letter from Henri."

"I thought I heard the postman come by," Alcide said.

"He did, and he had this. Henri, of course, had no idea about… what happened, when he wrote the letter," Seraphine said.

Alcide nodded, and said, "I'm sorry. I am sure he'll be notified."

"He probably has by now, but he didn't know when he wrote this. It is like a letter from a different time. When everything was still alright with us, and with the animals," she said.

Alcide was a bit surprised at the word "alright." Her husband had gone off to war, and the country was invaded. Even before the tragic loss of the baby, things had not been alright, but he didn't say anything.

"The Henri who wrote this letter is different from the one that is out there now. I know, because I am different. Now, the damaged Henri is going to come home to my damaged self," she said.

"Please," Alcide said, and then Esme whinnied loudly enough to startle him and Seraphine.

"Even the farm is damaged. And Elise is an orphan," Seraphine said.

"Esme isn't dead!" Olivier said.

"Might as well be," Seraphine said, and Esme snorted, ears pinned back, pawing.

"Don't say that," Olivier said.

"The horse has gone mad," Seraphine said, "And even the land. The field is changed. My baby is part of the soil out there now. My dead child is the land."

"You're the one who sounds mad," Olivier said.

Alcide said, "Olivier!"

Seraphine said, "Don't say that to me!"

"You said Esme might as well be dead, and that your baby is the land!" Olivier said.

"Get out! Go away, Olivier!" Seraphine said.

"We need him here," Alcide said.

"Well, he can leave until he learns some manners!" Seraphine said.

"What about Esme?" Olivier said.

"What about her? You get out of here!" Seraphine said.

"Olivier, I'll take care of her. Take a couple days off. She'll be fine, I promise," Alcide said.

"But…" Olivier started to say.

"Go," Seraphine said, turning to brush Elise.

Alcide watched as Olivier gave him one more look, and then he hugged Esme around the neck. "Watch out for her," Olivier said, and he walked out of the barn.

Alcide followed him, and Seraphine didn't say a word.

Once outside, Alcide said to Olivier, "Come back tomorrow, late in the afternoon. I'm sure she will cool down by then."

"Please don't let her do anything to the mare. Keep Esme safe. You promise?" Olivier asked.

"Go on. I promise. Come back tomorrow," Alcide said.

Olivier turned, and walked away. Alcide watched him go, and then he returned to the barn. Seraphine was with Elise, but it was clear she hadn't been there the entire time. Esme was in the breezeway, on crossties, unable to walk to her hay bag, or to turn, or even to lower her head.

"Why did you do this?" Alcide said, walking toward Esme.

"I don't trust her," Seraphine said, on her knees, hugging Elise.

Esme pulled at the ties, and stomped.

"Don't do this anymore. You upset the mare for nothing," Alcide said.

"Don't tell me what to do. You work for me," Seraphine said.

"Or else what? You'll send me away, too?" Alcide said.

He was almost to Esme, who was beside herself by this point, snorting, rearing up, tugging hard on the cross ties. As Alcide reached for the closer tie, it pulled free, and then the other let go. Esme reared again, and Alcide reflexively lifted his arm to shield his face. Esme did not charge at him, however, and instead spun and bolted out into the paddock.

"See? She's insane!" Seraphine said.

Catching his breath, Alcide said, "She wouldn't have been in such a state if you hadn't tied her."

"She was like that all along!" Seraphine said.

"If true, how did you manage to even get her on the cross ties?" Alcide said.

Seraphine said nothing, and turned back to Elise, hugging her tighter.

"You take care of Elise, and let me and the boy take care of everything else," Alcide said.

Seraphine still said nothing, and began to rock a bit, still holding Elise around the neck. Alcide stayed a moment longer, before going to check on Esme. The mare was in the paddock, bucking, snorting, farting, and rushing around. Alcide did have to admit, something had changed in the horse. They had said when he first arrived that she could be temperamental, but this horse was clearly upset.

16

◇◇◇◇◇

THE CAVE
1914

He sat on the evergreen branches, and even had a few across his lap. It wasn't that Olivier was especially cold, but they provided a sort of emotional comfort, and they smelled better than he did.

Olivier was whittling again. This time, the soft wood was obviously assuming the form of a human infant. He carved carefully, and slowly each shaved fragment of wood fell into the evergreen needles below.

"Make a baby, make a baby. Gently, gently," he said to himself.

He cut along the infant's back, the grain revealing a darker layer which was denser and more difficult to shape. Olivier chuckled, thinking of the literal stubborn streak in the wood, and said, "*Une belle pièce, seigneur, mais qui a un écart tenace.*" He smiled, and thought this was why a knife was better. The knife will take both the tougher and the softer layers at the same rate. Sandpaper would remove the softer wood, and leave the dense layer proud.

"Don't wear away at something, cut it off. Cut it," he said.

Cautiously, he removed soft and tough layers together, but only in the thinnest amounts. "It's not faster. It's right, it's even, but it's not faster," Olivier said.

A gust of wind swirled leaves at the mouth of the cave, and he looked that way to make sure that's all it was. Olivier sat quietly, not moving for a moment, and listened. Satisfied, he returned to his whittling.

"Make a baby. Careful, be careful when making babies," he said.

Turning the wood, he slowly rounded a little shoulder. "Making babies can make you crazy. Almost every time. Almost. Why? Wait, does it? Is it the baby's fault? Why? Maybe it is something the baby does? Or is it something the baby takes away?" he asked.

He put the carving and knife down, lifted bits of the evergreen branches from his legs, and walked out of the cave. Turning left, he walked just a little way to a stand of bushes, and urinated. "Does the sense leak out of them?" he asked.

He returned to the cave, but didn't sit right away. He looked down at the carving. "It can't be pulled by the baby on the way out. It can't be the baby's fault. Seraphine's baby died inside her. It wasn't born; it didn't grip her sanity, and pull it from her. But making babies crazes them somehow. They aren't right after. They aren't right," Olivier said.

He stopped whittling, cradled the miniature tree infant in his arms, and lay back on the bedding. A fresh smell of needles came up from beneath his head.

"Look how sad she was that her baby died. So upset, like she truly loved the baby, but she loves the foal now. How can that switch happen like that? She doesn't go out to the grave of her real baby. Mothers leave," he said, staring at the ceiling of the cave.

"Babies make themselves from their mothers. No, mothers make babies. Wait. Babies form, they grow. Does soil do work to make a plant? No, babies make themselves. They make their own bones by taking the mother's bones. They make their brains and their skin by taking from the mother's brain and flesh," he said.

He looked at the wood-baby, and said, "They suck the skin and bones off their mothers. But, wait, I just said, it's not the child's fault. Don't blame the baby. But what if the baby takes the mother's sanity as its own. What if babies strip the bones, the blood, and sense?"

Olivier sat up, and thought, *If that's true, then why would a mother love something that did that to her? Is it because she's supposed to? A mother loves her baby even when no one is there to judge her, right?*

Turning the carving in his hand, he said, "She loves. Love? They always say it's a different love. Is it love?

Or longing? Missing those parts taken from her? She longs for the parts that the baby took? Covets?"

Olivier picked up the knife and began to whittle again, "For some mothers, they can't bear it. Maybe they leave because the longing is too much. They miss that bone and blood too much."

17

◇◇◇◇◇

PARIS
1922

I asked Alcide, "What was wrong with the mare, Esme? Was she upset about being unable to nurse her foal?"

"She could have nursed the foal," Alcide said.

I wasn't familiar with such things, so I asked, "If the horse had milk, why give Elise goat milk? Why not just milk the horse?"

"That's a good way to get hurt, or even killed. A goat will let you milk them, happily. They'll get to a point where they will walk over for milking, without you even calling them. A mare is a different story. You've got to be under the horse, and she can cripple you with a single kick. People love horses, but they love them to be mild. I've seen a man get his head stoved in by a single kick. I once saw a woman, checking a horse's sore tooth, get three fingers taken off by a single bite. I won't ever try to milk a horse. Besides, there was more goat milk than we knew what to do with," Alcide said.

"So, maybe she was uncomfortable. Traumatized by the whole affair. Plus, the horse might have been sensing the state Seraphine was in," I said.

"I think that went into it, but there was something more," Alcide said.

I asked, "What else was there?"

Alcide was quiet for a moment, and then said, "There was something that seemed to hang over everything on the farm. You wanted to be free of it. It was like a net draped over all of us."

"You went mad?" I asked.

"Of course not!" Alcide said. "I am saying it was in the air. A blanket of fear, thick and terrible. And it was worse for Esme and Seraphine. They seemed more... affected."

"Having been pregnant?" I asked.

"They had that in common, but I don't know for sure why them," Alcide said. "That mare went bad."

"Surely, you don't believe an animal can be evil?" I asked.

"Have you ever heard of the le Drapé?" Alcide asked.

I leaned back, and said, "Drapery? Like curtains?"

"Or maybe le Drac?"

"I have not," I said, wishing he would get to some sort of point.

"There are many legends," Alcide said.

"Legends of the Cagots?" I said.

"I heard these stories as a boy, yes, but they are not only found with us. Across the south of France, all the way to Marseilles, they have these. You especially hear of le Drapé when you go farther east, but for us, the scary stories featured le Drac," Alcide said.

"What is it?"

"It depends on the story. Sometimes, it is an amphibious creature that can take the form of other animals, such as a rabbit, a lamb, or a horse," he said.

"A horse? Are you suggesting Esme?" I asked.

"Some stories even have them taking human form," Alcide said.

"What does this have to do with the farm?" I asked.

Alcide said, "These monsters would lure people, and take them away. Appearing as a beautiful white horse, they would pull people, often children, onto their backs. Once full, the monster's back, still looking like a horse, would get longer with each additional person. When the monster had enough people, it would run into the water, diving deep, usually into one of the larger rivers, with those people trapped on its back."

"So, they drowned people," I said.

"Not drowned. They could bring them down into submerged caves, where the people were held. Some of the stories had them eating the people they caught. Other versions have them capturing women whose breasts were full of milk, to use them as wet-nurses for the young of le Drac," Alcide said.

"The monsters had babies that needed breastfeeding?" I asked.

"Women breastfed those babies of le Drac for seven years, or so the stories say."

I was aghast at even the concept of a human baby breastfeeding until such an age. My own memory went back to around age four, so had I breastfed until age 7, that would mean three years of memories of nursing? And Alcide's tale was of breastfeeding a monster, which made it horrific.

"There is a version where a woman was washing clothes at the riverbank, and she was lured into the water by a bowl she saw floating by. Le Drac used to bait people into the water with things like that. She went in to get the bowl, and was pulled under and brought to its cave, where she was made to nurse its offspring. Some say there was air in the cave, others say she could breathe underwater while in there, but she could not see le Drac, until something got into her eye," Alcide said.

"What was it?" I asked.

"Some versions say a salve for the monster-baby's own eyes, others say oil from a meal of eels, but once she got the substance in her own eye, she could see the monster," Alcide said.

"And she nursed for seven years," I said.

"In most versions of the story, le Drac let her go after seven years, and she returned to her family, who welcomed her," Alcide said.

"So, it was a happy story in the end?" I asked.

"Not completely. You see, le Drac was on shore, among the people as a beautiful horse, but the woman could see, with that one anointed eye, that it was le Drac. She greeted him as such," Alcide said.

"Go on," I said.

"Le Drac was surprised, and asked with which eye she could see it. She told it that it was her right eye," Alcide said.

"Oh no," I said.

"Le Drac raised its hoof, that is what everyone else saw, but the woman saw it turn into a fierce claw that immediately took out her right eye. She screamed, fell to the ground, and the people all rushed to help her," Alcide said.

"How terrible," I said.

"And for the rest of her life, she was terrified of horses, and never spoke to another," Alcide said.

I nodded, and then asked, "So, what is the connection to Esme? You're not suggesting the mare was le Drac?"

"First, I am not the only one whose beliefs matter. What others believe is just as important. Second, an animal does not have to be completely one or the other, either completely honest, devoted, and kind, or are an evil monster dragging people to the depths. There are countless degrees in between. Finally, perhaps I am not limiting this to Esme," Alcide said.

I asked, "What about Elise? Could she have been the

one that went bad? With le Drac, which is worse? The monster desperate to feed its offspring and steals a wet-nurse from the dry world, or the young demon, hungrily thinking only of itself for seven years."

"The idea did come up," Alcide said.

18

◇◇◇◇◇

MONTAGNAT
1914

Alcide walked beside Seraphine, and Elise followed her, just as a foal would normally follow its mother.

"You should halter-break that one," Alcide said, and nodded toward Elise.

"She is too young," Seraphine said.

"We have no real control of her," Alcide said.

"I do," Seraphine said.

"Her mother is out here," Alcide said.

Seraphine's head whipped round to him, as if she might object to Esme being called Elise's mother, but then she said nothing, and they continued on. It was dusk as the three of them exited the barn and walked out into the paddock. At the corner was Esme, and away from her was Bijou, pulling at some grass at the base of a fencepost. Esme snorted, and lay her ears flat back.

"Easy now, Esme," Alcide said, "We won't come over there."

Elise stayed very close to Seraphine, and Esme stayed where she was. Bijou lifted her head, as if to survey the situation.

"Something is seriously wrong with that horse. The way she turned on the baby, throwing her down by her neck like that," Seraphine said.

"It happens. Mares sometimes reject their foals," Alcide said, but he knew she was right. He'd seen rejection several times, but this seemed different.

"She seemed angry with Elise," Seraphine said.

"When a mare won't nurse, it almost seems as if the whole idea scares her," Alcide said.

Seraphine said, "But this was not fear. She meant to hurt the baby. She seemed furious with her."

Esme's ears went straight up and forward, but not toward them. Instead, Esme was focused out toward the road. Alcide looked out that way, and saw Claire arriving with Suzanne. Esme snorted again. Claire and her daughter looked toward them all, and then Suzanne could be seen, shaking her head. Standing straighter, Claire brushed Suzanne's arm and nodded. She then left Suzanne on the edge of the road and headed for the paddock.

Esme whinnied and turned in place. She snorted and pinned her ears back once more. Elise seemed anxious, but never left Seraphine's side. As Claire came into the paddock and approached Alcide, Esme whinnied loudly.

"What in the world is wrong with that horse?" Claire asked.

"She rejected her foal, and has been off ever since," Alcide said.

"She hates Elise now," Seraphine said, and stroked the foal's neck.

Esme stomped and snorted, and shifted left and then right.

"Why did you come?" Seraphine asked.

Claire seemed surprised at the tone, and said, "I can't seem to find my camera. I wondered if I have left it here."

Esme whinnied again.

"I haven't seen it," Alcide said, never taking his eyes off Esme. The foal moved so that Seraphine was between her and the mare.

Esme shrieked and whinnied once more, and suddenly Suzanne started screaming from the edge of the road, repeatedly.

"Oh my God!" Claire said, and headed for Suzanne.

Esme whinnied, and Suzanne screamed. Esme whinnied again, and Suzanne screamed again. Claire got to Suzanne, wrapped an arm around her, and tried to turn her to head home. But when Esme whinnied once more, Suzanne answered again, and Esme reared.

"Get you and the filly back in the barn," Alcide said. Esme came down, and then bounced back into the air, rearing again each time her hooves came down.

"What are you going to do?" Seraphine asked.

"Get in the barn, I said," Alcide said. Seraphine walked into the barn and Elise followed, but they watched Esme the whole way in. Alcide came into the barn, too, and then walked past them.

"That animal should be put down," Alcide said, "Someone is going to get hurt. She's not right."

Seraphine said, "If you think that's best."

Alcide was astonished that she took it so calmly. She had been close with Esme; even Henri had said so. They began to distance themselves during the last weeks of their pregnancies, and then especially since that fateful night, there had been a break. Still, that she could so nonchalantly agree to Esme being destroyed surprised him.

"Are you sure?" Alcide asked.

Then Seraphine nodded and said, "Yes, put her down."

"No!"

They looked over to see Olivier coming in.

"Don't say that! You can't kill her," Olivier said.

"The horse isn't well," Alcide said.

"You didn't see. She was crazed. Ever since she tried to kill Elise," Seraphine said.

"What if she was right to?" Olivier asked.

"What did you say?" Seraphine asked.

"Who would know better than a mother? Maybe there is something evil about that thing!" Olivier said, pointing at Elise.

"The only evil is that horse out in the paddock!" Seraphine said.

Olivier ran by them and out. Alcide and Seraphine went after him, and Elise followed. Esme suddenly stood still, except for twitching in her shoulder muscles. Olivier stopped, and turned to face Alcide, with the mare behind him. Seraphine arrived then, and Elise cautiously approached.

"See? She is alright. How would you feel if you were separated from your foal?" Olivier asked.

"She gave up her baby. Elise is mine now," Seraphine said.

"Listen to yourself! That's a horse! Not a baby!" Olivier said, and took a few steps towards Elise. Seraphine rushed forward and stepped into his path, protecting the foal, and she pushed him hard. Not expecting it, Olivier fell to the ground. Esme immediately charged at Seraphine.

"Look out!" Alcide said, but could do nothing else.

Seraphine jumped out of the way, and was on one knee when Esme wheeled around, and struck out at Seraphine. The front hoof grazed Seraphine's face, cutting a gash in her cheek.

The foal moved away, and Alcide stepped forward to help Seraphine, but it was old Bijou who came between Esme and Seraphine. The heavier Bijou collided with Esme, sideswiping her away from Seraphine, protecting the kneeling and bleeding woman from another strike. Esme immediately bolted to the farthest part of the paddock. Bijou took a few steps before raising her head high, her eye barely visible in the fading light, breathing in great gusts, her tail swishing.

Alcide lifted Seraphine to her feet, saw the blood on her face, and hustled her back into the barn. Elise came up so tight to Seraphine that she almost took her off her feet as they went in. Alcide led them both into the large stall, and said, "Don't move! We'll take a look at the cheek in a moment." He then went around the corner, grabbed the rifle off the wall, checked to see if it was loaded, and headed for the paddock. When he came out of the barn, he was completely convinced he had to put Esme down. He had no doubt that she was going to kill someone eventually, but as he arrived in the paddock, he saw Olivier open the far gate.

"Olivier!" Alcide said.

Olivier said nothing. He slapped Esme on the rump, and she ran off into the dark. Olivier promptly closed the gate and walked straight at Alcide. The old man wasn't sure what Olivier was prepared to do, the boy's face was screwed up in rage, and Alcide was somewhat relieved when the boy walked right by him without a word. Alcide followed him into the barn. Olivier walked past Seraphine and Elise without a glance, and left the barn without looking back.

Alcide turned to Seraphine, whose cheek and neck were covered in blood. "Let's go clean that up in the house," Alcide said.

"What about Elise?" Seraphine asked.

"The mare is gone. Leave Elise, and we'll get that bleeding stopped. You can come back after," Alcide said.

Seraphine hugged Elise, leaving blood on the foal's forehead, and then Alcide led her into the house.

19

◇◇◇◇◇

MONTAGNAT
1914

A letter from Henri

It was a couple days later, as Alcide walked toward the goat pen, that the wind carried a sheet of paper into his path. Picking it up, Alcide saw it was a new letter from Henri.

He looked back toward the house, and then looked off into the field, before he began to read it:

"My Dear Seraphine,

I am heartbroken, as I know you must be, to learn of the loss of our child. While surrounded by misery here, I have had thoughts only of life, of our lives together, at home. Now, I want only to be there with you, to comfort you, and to assure you that there will be happier years to come. We will have children and, soon enough, you and I will walk alongside Esme, our child high on her back, each of us holding her hand."

Alcide looked up at the sky, and thought, *Any horse in their future would not be Esme.*

The letter continued:

"The sun will be on our faces, a crop of oats standing tall in the field, and you can make one of your pies. Everyone has challenges, Seraphine, and it seems we are having all of ours at once. Stay strong for us. Keep faith in me, and in our Lord that this war will soon end, and we won't be parted again."

Alcide wondered if he should write to Henri, to explain how things had changed on the farm, and to prepare him, but then thought better of it. It was not his farm, it was not his marriage, and it was not his place.

Besides, the letter probably would not get there in time, and Henri would find out soon enough:

"I have been granted leave to come to you. By the time you receive this, you can expect me in less than a week, depending how things go here. They have given me twenty-four hours, in addition to the time it takes to travel. How I long to hold you, to feel your face against mine, and to hear your voice. I will be there soon. You will see. I love you. —Henri"

Alcide hung his head. As sad as it was on the farm, he knew it was about to get more so. Tragedy is bad enough, but the wreckage left by misfortune is often worse, and longer lasting. Outsiders would think the loss of the baby would be the worst of it, but Alcide knew that every time her death came to mind, it would be like a fresh cut, and a new blow. He knew that worse than "she is dead" was "she is still dead."

Movement caught the corner of his eye, and Alcide saw Seraphine come out of the house, with her facial injury caused by Esme still clearly visible, and head for the barn. Her gaze fell to his hands, and the letter. Alcide immediately let it go, and allowed the wind to carry it away. Seraphine didn't say a word, but instead she entered the barn, and Alcide had no doubt she was returning to Elise.

20

◇◇◇◇◇

PARIS
1922

Alcide suddenly turned to me, hands on the table, and said, "She began to fall apart. Not simple grief, which I know well. Something seriously wrong was developing. She was in obvious decline."

"Seraphine was, you mean?" I asked.

"Each night was colder than the last, and yet she began sleeping in the barn," Alcide said.

"With you?" I asked.

Alcide was clearly taken aback, and said, "With the foal, you idiot. I was up in the loft, where I had been, but she was below, with Elise. I would walk through, on my way to the ladder, and she would be standing and cradling its head, swaying on her feet, as if rocking a baby."

"And she slept out there?" I asked.

"In the hay. Sometimes, the foal was lying next to her,

but regardless, Seraphine no longer slept in the house," Alcide said.

"That is odd," I said.

"She would sing to Elise, too. Do you know the lullaby, '*La Sainte Vierge*'? She would sing it again and again. Sometimes, she wept as she sang it," Alcide said.

I asked, "You could hear her? From the loft?"

Alcide shifted his weight a bit, and then said, "I could hear from my bedding in the loft, yes, but sometimes I came to the edge, to hear better. Sometimes, to look down, only to see if she was alright."

I asked, "Wasn't someone expected to be in the barn, overnight, for the feedings?"

"I had been feeding the foal in the middle of the night, but then, one day, she said she would do it. When I declined her offer, and said she needed her sleep, she said she would sleep better if she could be close to Elise," Alcide said.

"At least she didn't try to bring the foal into the house," I said, and laughed.

Alcide's face froze hard. "This is not the least bit funny. I am telling you, the woman seemed to be going mad, and not simply grief-stricken," he said.

"To be honest, so far, it does sound more like grief. Perhaps a bit of obsession to make up for her lost child, but not insanity," I said.

Alcide said, "It became necessary for me to go into the house, to get her some food, or else she wouldn't eat."

"Seraphine, you mean?" I asked, and immediately felt foolish. He only stared at me in response, until I asked, "You fed her three times per day?"

"It was more like I fed her a little bit, but all day long. A piece of bread until there was no more, or a slice of cheese. When I cooked, I made her an egg and maybe a potato," Alcide said.

"And she lived on only that?" I asked.

"She wanted nothing more. Just a little food, water, and milk," Alcide said.

"She was drinking the goat milk, too?" I asked.

He paused a moment, and nodded. I followed this with, "Were you running out of milk? Were the goats able to produce enough?"

"More than enough," Alcide said.

"But, Seraphine, she didn't want anything else? Like a piece of pie, or a glass of wine, or anything? Bread and potatoes, sleeping in the cold barn, and singing to a foal. Perhaps that is more than extreme grief," I said.

Alcide walked away from the table and looked down at the street. A dog barked in the distance, and a few pigeons landed on the terrace.

"There is something else," he said, and I waited without making a sound.

The pigeons strutted beneath the little table, perhaps looking for crumbs.

"I was in the loft one night, and it was quite cold. I heard a sound; it was sort of a groaning, really. It woke me, and my thoughts were muddled at first. Then, I realized it was Seraphine, and I was sure she was hurt," he said.

"Groaning?" I asked.

"She was making sounds I'd never heard from her before—soft sobs, mixed with moans and whispers. Maybe she had fallen, I thought, and was lying below unable to get up, or call for help," Alcide said.

The distant dog barked again, and one pigeon flew away.

"What had happened to her?" I asked.

Alcide looked down, and scanned from his left to his right. He said, "I slowly walked to the edge of the loft, and looked down."

"Was it too dark to see?" I asked.

"She had a lantern, set so low it was flickering, and she had pulled her garment off her shoulders. It hung around her waist, and her bare back was to me," Alcide said. He stopped, and straightened, as if it pained him to continue.

"What is it? She was just standing in the barn that way?"

"She was bent forward at the waist, and even by the lantern light, it was difficult to see what was in her hands," Alcide said.

I asked, "What was it?"

Alcide said, "Seraphine stood a bit straighter. Her sobs were mixed with gasps, and groans of pain, and yet she kept whispering, 'Yes' and 'That's right' again and again. She slowly extended her arms straight out to her sides, her palms slightly upturned."

Thoroughly confused, I asked, "Was she praying?"

Alcide turned to face me, and said, "She was feeding the foal. I could see in the flickering light, that the filly was nursing from Seraphine's breast." Alcide turned away, and again looked down in the street.

I couldn't believe it. "Is that even possible?" I asked.

"Certainly, with puppies, and even deer, I had heard of it. Somewhere, long ago, I thought I remembered a story of a foal nursing that way," Alcide said, "But I was not prepared for the sight of it."

"What did you do?" I asked.

"Once the image had sunk in, and once the shock of the moment had passed and I believed my eyes, I backed away as silently as I could, and returned to my bedding in the hay," Alcide said.

"You didn't stop her?" I asked.

"Just the opposite. I felt I had intruded on something so incredibly personal, no matter how insane it seemed. There was all at once pain and passion, grief and giving, and spirituality, and I felt so singularly unworthy to be in the same space, that I could not make myself small enough, nor quiet enough. The blood in my ears sounded loud and intrusive in her space. I thought of my own dear wife, lost that terrible day, all those years ago, here in Paris. I thought of the pain I felt at losing them both, but I knew the pain would have been all the worse if she and I had shared the loss of our daughter," Alcide said.

"Worse? Losing one would've been worse than losing both?" I asked.

"My wife never had to suffer the loss. They went to Paradise together. My pain was mine alone, and I managed it, sequestered it," Alcide said.

"Go on," I said.

"Had she survived and we had been together, mourning our daughter, I would've had to have watched her agony while trying to tie off my own pain… we would've multiplied each other's grief," Alcide said.

"People always talk of others comforting them in times of sorrow," I said.

"It's nonsense. We amplify each other's pain when we share it. It is not like carrying a heavy thing, where more hands make it lighter," Alcide said.

"It isn't?"

"Not at all. Instead, grief is like screaming into the dark. The more voices, the louder. One is less conspicuous, less an individual, but the work is not shared. It is more intense, not less," he said, "Words and platitudes do not help. They only force the grieving person to participate in ritual thanking, hugs of gratitude, when really they wish to retreat and try to sort out their lives."

"I thought they were sincerely grateful," I said.

"In deep grief, we're too stricken to be anything but

wooden. Like wooden carvings of ourselves. Have you ever looked deeply into the eyes of someone who has just lost someone so dear? It is like he or she is not even in that face, in that mind," Alcide said.

Not knowing what else to say, I asked, "So, you were seeing Seraphine's grief and you did what?"

"With Henri gone to war, and Seraphine's state of mind… she was nursing a foal! From her own breasts! There was nothing I could do to help. And did she even need aid? I didn't know what to do," Alcide said.

"And her husband was returning," I said.

"And I knew I would have to tell him that I was in the loft, watching his wife, who was nude from the waist up, breastfeeding a horse," Alcide said.

"Why did you tell him?"

"He needed to know to whom he was married," Alcide said.

"When did he return?"

Alcide said, "Two days after, around midday."

21

◇◇◇◇◇

MONTAGNAT
1914

When Alcide spotted Henri walking down the road toward the farm, in uniform, with his bundle hanging from a strap slung over his shoulder, he did not walk toward him. Alcide thought that every additional second that it took for the two men to come together would be another moment that Henri would not know how bad things had gotten.

Henri's long pale blue overcoat was open, and he wore no cap. It was clear that Henri had not taken the time for a haircut, nor did it look like he had bathed. His boots were caked with mud as he came toward the barn, and stopped in front of Alcide. The two men shook hands, and their faces were grim.

"Welcome home," Alcide said.

"I can only stay until tomorrow. My unit is on the line, and it was damn fine of them to let me come back even for this long," Henri said.

"I hope the fighting will end soon," Alcide said.

Henri nodded, but gave no sign of having the same hope. He looked around and asked, "Where is Seraphine?"

"In the barn, but maybe we should talk first," Alcide said.

Henri looked toward the barn, and said, "Right after I let her know that I am here."

Alcide stared at his feet for a moment as Henri headed toward the barn, but then he followed the younger man.

As Henri entered the barn, he called out, "Seraphine?"

Alcide followed him inside, and said, "We should talk."

Elise whinnied, but Seraphine did not respond to her husband. Henri and Alcide walked farther in, and then they spotted her, standing straight, and right beside Elise the foal.

Alcide saw the first sign of a smile wash across Henri's face, and he said, "Seraphine. My God, it's good to see you."

Seraphine said nothing, and didn't take a step toward him. Henri's smile fell slowly, and he approached her. "My God! What happened to your face!"

Her face still had bruising and a scab from where Esme had struck her with a hoof.

"Esme did that," Alcide said.

"Are you okay? Come into the light, so I can see," Henri said, and he gently pulled on her arm.

"No," she said.

Henri froze a moment, and then asked, "What is it? Why not, Seraphine?" He pulled at her elbow once more, a bit more emphatically. Despite her best effort, Henri pulled her a step forward, and then Alcide and Henri saw that she had her fingers in Elise's mane.

Henri said, "Come on! Let me see your face."

"No! Leave me alone!" Wrenching free of Henri's grip and returning to Elise, she wrapped her arms around the horse's neck and fell to her knees.

Henri turned back to Alcide, and asked, "What is going on?"

"I tried to warn you," Alcide said.

"Warn me?" Henri said, and then stepped toward Seraphine and Elise. Seraphine didn't say anything, really, so much as she growled at him, and with wild eyes. Henri stopped abruptly. Alcide put his hand in the middle of Henri's back and guided him to a distant corner of the barn.

"She has become quite attached to the foal, and she is not available to anyone else," Alcide said.

"This started when the baby died?" Henri asked.

"She's been sleeping out here, and I bring her food," Alcide said.

Henri rubbed his face with both hands, and looked over at Seraphine, but then he looked in every direction, and asked, "Where is Esme?"

"Esme had taken a turn, too, and the night that she attacked Seraphine, I had taken it into my mind to put the animal down. Olivier stepped in, however, and saved Esme by setting her loose into the woods. I have not been able to find her, and we've not seen Olivier since that night either," Alcide said.

"Jesus, Alcide, you were hired to prevent chaos here," Henri said.

Alcide knew it was all too much for Henri, and took a soft tone when he said, "No one could have prevented all of this, or foreseen it. Your baby was stillborn, and Esme became unstable. As did Seraphine," Alcide said.

"Seraphine? What else has she done, beside sleeping in the barn?" Alcide said.

Alcide hesitated, as if unsure of a way to tell him. He looked Henri in the eye, and wondered how much he could take. Alcide searched the rafters for a moment, and a bird flew from one set of shadows to another.

"Tell me," Henri said.

"I was sleeping in the loft, when I was awakened by a sound. When I looked down, I saw Seraphine. She was…"

Henri asked, "Was what?"

"She was nursing the foal. Herself," Alcide said.

Henri grabbed both of Alcide's arms, and the men's eyes locked. It was as if Henri was begging Alcide to take it back. He didn't. Henri released Alcide and walked quickly over to Seraphine.

Not sure what Henri would do, Alcide was right beside him when he pulled Seraphine to her feet. She groaned, but didn't fight. Seraphine stood perfectly still, with her arms down by her sides, and Henri opened her coat. Beneath, the men could see that her white shirt was stained with milk and blood. Alcide watched Henri search Seraphine's face for any sign that she was still inside there, but she remained impassive. Henri opened her shirt in full view of Alcide, who, at the sight of the bruised and bloodied breasts, turned away.

Henri said, "You've gone mad. You are a woman, and this is a farm animal!"

Seraphine suddenly pushed Henri away with both hands, and then immediately lunged at him, shrieking, and hitting him.

Alcide had no idea Olivier had been there and watching, but just then the boy came out of Bijou's stall, ran by them, and out of the barn. Seraphine went silent and limp, and fell into the straw.

Henri, gasping, said, "Alcide, follow that boy and see if he knows where Esme is."

"But what about…?" Alcide said.

"I'll look after her. Go, don't lose him," Henri said.

22

◇◇◇◇◇

THE CAVE
1914

Olivier knew that he had not been careful, and he could hear Alcide behind him in the woods. It wasn't that he wanted the cave to be found, but he simply didn't care in the moment. He only wanted to get out of the barn, away from the shouting and the fighting, and that foal watching it all. Olivier entered the cave, sat, and waited to see if the old man would find it. Maybe it was time for something to change.

However, when Alcide did peer into the cave, Olivier had a flash of dread. Suzanne knew about it, but she hadn't shown anyone. The old man was different from most people, too, but Olivier was unsure.

"Are you coming in?" Olivier asked.

Alcide was clearly startled at the sound, and it seemed to take him a minute to fix Olivier's exact location.

"I've only come because he wants to know where

Esme is. He sent me to follow only to find the mare," Alcide said.

"You were going to shoot her. Why should I tell you?" Olivier said.

"He's the owner, and wants her back. I certainly wouldn't harm her now," Alcide said.

"She's not in here," Olivier said.

"I can see that," Alcide said.

Olivier walked across the cave, from one set of shadows to another. He saw Alcide glance at his carvings. Olivier said, "It's all the foal's fault, you know that?"

"What is? Esme attacking the woman?" Alcide asked.

"All of it. Esme's fear. The woman's madness," Olivier said.

"What are you talking about?" Alcide asked.

"When I was about ten years old, my father died. We also had a foal then. It was a very difficult time. My mother, like the Arsenault woman, went insane. She blamed me for my father's lungs failing him. Even before he died, he would cough blood, and my mother would say he never did that before I was born. After he was gone, whenever I was there, she would tell me how I was to blame," Olivier said.

"That is terrible, but you know it cannot be true," Alcide said.

"What is truer than what a mother tells her child? There is nothing more true, even if the child knows the mother is mad," Olivier said.

Olivier sat, and Alcide asked, "What happened next? How long did you stay?"

"Until she tried to kill me," Olivier said.

"Your mother tried to kill you?"

"With a pillow. I was sleeping, and woke to a pillow over my face, and her lying on top of it. I could not breathe. Kicking and swinging my arms, I could not move her," Olivier said.

Alcide was silent.

"I am not making this up," Olivier said.

"I believe you. How did you survive?"

"Instead of kicking and pushing, I began pinching. Can you imagine it? I pinched and pinched. Not one long pinch, but hard pinches, many of them, everywhere I could grab. I was beginning to see stars, but I pinched as hard as I could, as fast as I could, and as often as I could. I could hear her screaming each time, until she jumped off me. As I came out from under that pillow, sitting up and desperate for air, I saw her running away. She ran right out of the house," Olivier said.

"You pinched?" Alcide asked.

Olivier said, "Want me to show you?" He stood up, willing to pinch the old man to demonstrate.

"I don't," Alcide said. "Where did she go?"

"I never found out. I thought she might return with something more dangerous than a pillow, so I packed a few things, grabbed a loaf of bread, and left. As I was leaving, there was that foal. It was silent, and staring at me.

It never moved a muscle," Olivier said.

"But the foal had nothing to do with what your mother did to you," Alcide said.

"My mother had been spending a lot of time with that foal. Even when my father was too sick to get out of bed, and he would have to call to her, to call her in from that animal. She would give him a drink of water, or clean him, and then she would go straight back to the baby horse," Olivier said.

"She couldn't just sit beside him all day," Alcide said.

"She never sat with him. At the end, even when she was in the same room, she wouldn't even talk to him. My mother would answer anything he asked her, with as few words as possible," Olivier said.

"And you think that was the foal's fault?"

"Now that we have seen what that foal did here, to this woman, I wonder is it a coincidence? Young girls are all in love with horses, and then as women, they are all in love with foals," Olivier said.

"So, you blame adult horses, too? Why save Esme then?" Alcide asked.

"I do not blame all horses. But I have seen, twice now, the witchy ways of foals. I don't trust them at all," Olivier said.

Alcide said nothing for a moment, and then asked, "You left home."

"I never went back," Olivier said.

"Where did you go?" Alcide asked.

Olivier sat back down, and said, "I went from farm to farm, sleeping in lofts like you are. I was small, but I learned that if you work hard, and keep out of people's secrets, you can get along. Something you haven't learned, it seems."

"You know nothing about me," Alcide said.

Olivier said, "One day, I found this." He motioned in a circle to the cave.

"It must be cold. We could at least bring a bit of straw, instead of pine boughs," Alcide said.

"See, already you want to change it. It's fine, and it's mine," Olivier said.

Alcide was quiet, and then he, too, sat. "Olivier, he wants to know where the mare, where Esme, is. Do you know? It is rightfully his horse. In fact, you saved his horse for him."

"I certainly did not save that horse for him. I saved Esme from you, and the woman, and from that foal," Olivier said.

"Do you know where she is right now?" Alcide asked.

"When she ran off into the dark that night, I thought I'd seen the last of her," Olivier said.

"But you saw her again."

"The next day, I found her at the cliff. Do you know it?" Olivier said, "She was right at the edge, looking this way and that, and down."

Alcide said, "She was trapped."

Olivier said, "Hardly. She was deciding."

"Making a choice?"

"On whether to jump to her death or not," Olivier said.

Alcide shifted and said, "Come on now. Animals will avoid death instinctively, but they have no concept that they will someday die themselves. The don't know that they can choose to die."

"How do you know? Animals know they will die someday. Animals know when they are dying of illness," Olivier said.

"Nonsense."

"I believe animals even know when a person intends to kill them, even in mercy. Animals have much more grace than we do. They know when we are going to end their lives as an act of mercy, and they allow it. Out of grace, and trust," Olivier said.

"You're barely a man, and I've lived a long life. I have known animals to be kind, and clever, and smart. Especially dogs and horses. But I've never seen any proof of an animal aware of death and choosing it," Alcide said.

"I am young, but life ages us differently. Your age gives you patience that I don't have, but my life, and all the hours alone, have given me time to work things out in my head. Most people are too busy to think," Olivier said.

Alcide gave a big sigh, and Olivier felt like Alcide might be seeing him for the first time. Alcide then asked, "Olivier, did the mare go over the cliff?"

"She didn't. I talked to her for over an hour, with her hooves at the rim. Finally, she turned, gave me a sniff one last time, and walked away," Olivier said.

"Do you know where she went?" Alcide asked.

Olivier shifted, looked like he might say where she was, but then said, "I did not follow her, and I haven't seen Esme since," Olivier said.

Alcide nodded, and said, "I'll tell Arsenault that. Thank you for telling me."

Olivier said, "Watch out for that foal."

"What do you mean?"

"The foal, Elise, is a spirit that has taken control of Seraphine. Maybe the foal even killed the baby to take its place in the woman's heart," Olivier said.

"Don't say that. If you ever return to the farm, you must not say such things," Alcide said.

"What if it's true? That night with the lightning, all that energy in the air. Was the witch howling in the field? I've seen her do that in storms, before you came," Olivier said.

"Are you blaming dumb Suzanne for the baby being stillborn, too?" Alcide asked.

"The witch fights darkness that only she can see. I think she was trying to save the baby. The lightning was of the earth, not the sky. Suzanne was trying to save the baby, and I think the spirit which wanted to be in the baby, ended up in the foal, but not before silencing the child out of spite. It was denied the baby so it killed the child, took the foal instead, and then stole the woman from our world," Olivier said.

"Do you know how insane you sound?" Alcide asked.

"Can you explain this world, without magic?" Olivier asked.

"I can explain it without demons, yes," Alcide said.

"People are the only demons. The magic that works against us, you would call 'evil'," Olivier said.

"If it's not evil, what would you call it?"

"Nature," Olivier said.

Alcide only blinked at him, and then licked his lips.

"Go back to the farm," Olivier said.

"Will you ever return?" Alcide asked.

Olivier thought for a moment, and then asked, "How long will Arsenault stay? Before he goes back to the war?"

"He leaves tomorrow."

Olivier took a deep breath, and said, "I will come early in the morning, and see."

Alcide turned to leave, without saying another word.

Olivier said, "Make no promises to me, but I'm asking you not to tell anyone about where I stay."

Alcide nodded, and left.

Olivier moved over to the pile of evergreen branches, and laid down on them. He thought perhaps he should pack and leave immediately, because Arsenault may come out this way looking for the mare, and then stumble upon the cave. However, Olivier decided to stay. It was not time to leave yet.

23

◇◇◇◇◇

MONTAGNAT
1914

The next morning Olivier arrived, Alcide noticed, very early indeed. Perhaps Olivier felt guilty about missing Henri's previous sendoff. Together, Alcide and Olivier followed behind Henri as he entered the barn. He was clean-shaven this morning, and his hair had been brushed.

Alcide watched as Henri approached the stall where Seraphine, in her long, black coat, was bent beside Elise, and brushing her. Looking down at his wife, Henri said, "Seraphine."

She did not straighten, or even look up at him. She simply continued to brush Elise.

"Seraphine, it is time for me to return to my unit now," Henri said.

She stopped brushing for a moment, but then resumed, without saying a word. Henri said, "I do not know when I might return home. Don't you want to at least wish me well? To perhaps say a prayer?"

Without pausing the brushing, she said, "Be well, Henri."

Alcide saw Henri's face darken, and he suddenly lunged forward, and pulled Seraphine closer. Her upper arms were wrapped in his fingers, as he began to shake her back and forth, shouting, "You understand that I might never return? You understand I could die? You can't so much as give me a respectable goodbye? I am your husband, Seraphine!"

Her face was completely without emotion. As Henri jerked her forward and back, her head rocked violently, but her face never changed. As if it was made of stone. She didn't make a sound.

"Come out of it, dammit!" Henri shouted.

Alcide stepped forward, and grabbed Henri's shoulders, and said, "That's enough! Stop! That's enough."

Henri froze, stared at Seraphine, his face contorted, and then let her go. He turned, and took a couple steps, but had to stop because Olivier was blocking his way out of the barn. The boy looked up into Henri's face for a moment before he stepped aside, and let the man pass without saying a word. Henri left the barn, and was gone.

Alcide looked Seraphine over, and asked, "Are you alright?"

Seraphine took a few, slow steps backward.

"Seraphine?"

"Did he injure her?" Olivier asked.

"I don't think so," Alcide said.

"I have never seen him so angry," Olivier said.

"That was not the same man I came to this farm with," she said.

"Life has been hard on you both," Alcide said.

"He's not the same man," she said.

"He was hurt, and angry. He is returning to the war, and was likely scared he'd never see you again."

"My Henri was always so calm, so gentle. My Henri would have never done that."

Alcide said, "He, and you, have never faced these sorts of challenges before," Alcide said.

"I'm telling you, I looked in his eyes, and Henri wasn't in there," she said.

"Fine. But maybe when he returns, you all can be restored. This farm will bring your Henri back to you," Alcide said, although he wasn't sure he believed it.

"We did not inherit this farm, you know. We found it together, intentionally."

"I did not know."

"We felt lucky, and we bought it. Henri and I combined what money we had, my money had been left to me by my grandfather, and we bought this farm," she said, still seemingly emotionless.

Alcide glanced over at Olivier, who was standing still, with his hands at his sides, staring at Seraphine.

"That's a lot of money," Alcide said. "No government

loan?" His voice was kind, but it was clear that learning more about the farm was not his primary concern.

"We purchased it outright, but it wasn't that much. The man who owned it, and lived here before us, did not ask very much for it. In fact, the price was so low that Henri immediately asked if something was wrong with the house, the barn, land, or the water. The man took us for a walk, and we looked for ourselves," she said.

"He lived here alone?"

"He was alone when we bought it, but I don't know if he had always been," she said.

"Did he say if it had been a family farm?"

Seraphine said, "It wasn't a family farm. He said that he had bought it from someone else, and that it had been a bargain for him as well, so he was able to sell it for less than what he could have gotten for it."

"But why sell it for less? Why not get the most you can for it?"

She said, "He wanted nothing more to do with it. He said that he needed to get away."

"And the animals were here?"

"Bijou was here, and some goats. Soon after we bought the farm, a woman came with that crazy horse, Esme, and asked if she could pay us to board her here. We agreed, but we never saw her again," Seraphine said, showing the first bit of sadness.

Olivier said, "That horse is not crazy."

Alcide waved him off and asked, "So, a man sold you

a farm cheap, and a woman abandoned a young mare here? Don't you think that's odd?"

"He said it was on an energy line," she said.

"An energy line?" Alcide asked.

Seraphine took a couple more steps, and leaned against a railing. She sighed and said, "He wasn't really a farmer. He told us had been doing research with a British partner, who was an amateur archaeologist. They were exploring ideas."

Alcide asked, "But what is this energy line?"

"They, he and his partner, believed that there are lines that run across the lands, across borders and oceans, and they have a power to them. He said ancient sites are on those lines, and that they had some sort of magic," she said.

"Are you a believer in the occult?" Alcide asked.

"He didn't tell us much more, except he wanted to get off this land," she said.

"And that's why you got a good price?"

"Now I understand why. Look at all the tragedy that has come," she said.

"But at first, everything was fine," Alcide said.

"Weird things began happening. Things would go missing. Sometimes I wondered if it was him, stealing," she said, pointing at Olivier, "but then even he would have his own items disappear."

Alcide looked at Olivier, who slowly nodded.

"So, you believe that the land is cursed?" Alcide asked.

Seraphine turned to face Alcide straight on, and said, "I believe that everyone I love is being taken from me. All I have left is Elise."

"Henri will be back," Alcide said, and then regretted it.

"He's no longer my Henri," she said.

24

◇◇◇◇◇

MONTAGNAT
1914

A letter from Henri

Henri's visit had been a disaster, but in the coming weeks, he continued to write. Alcide saw it as a sign of love and hope, on Henri's part.

The ground was covered in an inch of fresh snow, and it continued to fall. A letter arrived two days before All Saints' Day, just before dusk. Alcide had been working with the goats, when the postman came. Taking the letter from the postman, Alcide thanked him. Olivier appeared moments later, stepping out of the trees.

"Is that a new coat?" Alcide asked Olivier.

"It isn't stolen," Olivier said.

Alcide said nothing more about the coat. As for the letter from Henri, as he had before, Alcide took the letter to Seraphine. She, as before, refused to take it. Instead, she continued to stroke Elise's face, and to feed the foal a bit of grain from her hand. The long black coat she wore was soiled, and her hair was more matted in a ball than it was tied on her head.

Alcide was eager for the foal to wean, perhaps in another month. It was not something he discussed with Seraphine. Alcide milked the goats, and labelled much of it for Elise. Most of it disappeared; some days more was consumed than others. Seraphine still slept in the barn with the foal, but Alcide made sure to never look down from the loft at night again.

He walked away from Seraphine, but was still in the barn when he opened the letter. With Olivier standing behind him, he began to read it aloud to them both:

"My dear wife,

It saddens me that my letters go unanswered, but I certainly take part of the blame for how we left things. I believe that we can return to living as we once did, if you'll only give us a chance. We can let everything that has happened remain in the past. We can start anew, perhaps with a long walk through the meadows. The confusion of these times can be left out there, and we can return to our home as fresh as newlyweds. With the depth of…"

"Watch out!" Olivier said.

Seraphine had suddenly appeared, and she pushed Alcide. Her teeth were bared, and she screamed at him, "Stop! Enough! I don't want another word from those letters heard in this barn, ever! Do you understand! That is a letter from a man I don't know, and to a woman I cannot believe I ever bore any resemblance to! It is a fantasy wrapped in a lie! Never read anything like that in here again!"

Seraphine stopped shouting, and Alcide stood there, saying nothing in return.

"Is that clear? I hear one more word from that man, and it will certainly be the worse for you!" she said, grabbing the riding crop off a hook, and she took a step toward him.

Elise whinnied.

"Calm yourself," Alcide said.

"I will not! If you even mention him to me again, you'll have no place here! Can I be clearer than that? I don't even know why you stay!" Seraphine said, her face was dark red, and her eyes wide. She was mere inches from Alcide's face at this point, and Olivier opened his coat. She looked over at him, and Alcide turned to see what he was pulling out. It was Claire's camera. He lifted it, as if to take a photograph of Seraphine in her rage, but before he could, Elise screamed, and ran past them and out of the barn. Seraphine ran after her. Olivier chased Seraphine with the camera held high. Alcide reached the boy just as they stepped outside the barn, but too late to stop Olivier from taking a photo. Looking in the direction the camera had been pointed, Alcide saw Seraphine chasing the foal into the old, unused half-paddock alongside the barn.

When Alcide turned back, Olivier was running off into the half-light, holding the camera in front of him with both hands.

25

◇◇◇◇◇

PARIS
1922

Alcide was standing there, his eyes glazed over at the memory of it all.

"Why did Olivier take a photo?" I asked.

Alcide pointed to the photograph on the table, and said, "He took this one."

"But why did he take it? He was trying to take a photo of the woman as she yelled at you. Why?" I asked.

Alcide took a deep breath, and said, "Maybe he was trying to capture something, to have proof of something."

"That she was crazy? Proof of the effect of an 'energy line?'" I asked.

"Perhaps to have proof that she had changed. To prove a physical change in her," Alcide said.

"Have proof to show whom?" I asked. "Was it intended to show that the foal had changed her?"

"What broke that woman was the death of her own

baby. Maybe Olivier was trying to understand his own mother. Maybe he saw a change in his mother when his father died, and he was hoping to capture the change in Seraphine in a photo, and trying to prove to himself that he hadn't imagined it."

"To prove she was crazy, or to prove to himself that he wasn't?" I asked.

Alcide shrugged, and then said, "Seraphine and Olivier were troubled people, both with good reason. And who am I to say? More than two decades later, I'm still mourning. Crazy? Insane? What is sanity? Is one required to be predictable in order to be considered sane? Or must one know the difference between good and evil? Everyone you might have thought crazy knew the difference between right and wrong."

I said, "So, if he wasn't crazy, Olivier was certainly troubled."

Alcide said, "And that was when it became clear that Olivier had stolen Claire's camera. Honestly, I thought she had misplaced it, or that her daughter had taken it out and left it in the forest or some field somewhere."

"Did you go to the cave to get the camera?" I asked.

"I stayed with Seraphine. We collected the foal, and she returned to the stall with Elise. She barely spoke, at least she did not speak to me. She mumbled under her breath, and sometimes, I think she growled. It was cold that night, or maybe it felt especially so because of the snow. The next day, the snow melted in an early-

November rain, leaving mud everywhere," Alcide said.

I asked, "So, when did you go to the cave to retrieve Claire's camera? That next day? Or did you ever?"

"I did not go right away. The next day, rain came, and with it, some hard news," Alcide said.

26

◇◇◇◇◇

MONTAGNAT
1914

The priest should have brought Claire Voisine with him, Alcide thought, but he arrived alone. Perhaps it really would not have mattered. Father Benoit went to the house, naturally thinking that Seraphine would be in there, but of course she was not.

The priest's knocking on the house door brought Alcide out of the barn.

"She is in here," Alcide called over to the priest.

"Ah, I see," said Father Benoit. He walked slowly through the mud, blinking at the rain, toward Alcide and the barn.

When he was closer, Alcide asked, "Something has happened to Henri?"

"I am afraid so. Very sad. That brave young man has gone to meet his Savior. He was killed yesterday, or the day before," Father Benoit said.

"They are not sure?" Alcide asked.

"It is terrible there, the fighting, the situation is very chaotic, I am told," Father Benoit said.

"When will the casket arrive?" Alcide asked.

"There will be no casket. They are burying any remains they find, of fallen men, in nearby soil. New cemeteries," he said.

Alcide asked, "Remains they find? They have not found him?"

"It's often that way," the priest said.

"Then perhaps he is not dead," Alcide said.

"Alcide, while it's true some men simply go missing, in this case, his comrades saw him killed. They collected pieces of him. He will be given a holy and proper burial."

"I see," Alcide said.

Father Benoit sighed and said, "It falls to me to tell his widow. Let's get out of this rain," Father Benoit said.

The two men entered the barn, and Alcide said, "I should prepare you. She has behaved strangely since the stillbirth, and has become obsessed with a foal."

"How tragic," Father Benoit said, shaking the rain from his arms, but never slowed his walk, and the two men were soon at the stall. When they found Seraphine, she looked over at the priest.

"Hello, Seraphine," Father Benoit said.

"Is he dead?" Seraphine said, her eyes locked on the priest.

"God's will, I'm afraid. Henri is at peace," he said.

As Alcide watched Seraphine, he had no idea what she would do or say next. At first, she said nothing, and simply stepped sideways until her hip was against Elise.

"Seraphine?" the priest asked.

She began to shrink. Her face twisted, her knees bent slowly, and she doubled over little by little, until she sat in a ball, hugging herself, beside the foal. Her teeth exposed, eyes searching left and right, fingers moving, but her arms were still wrapped around herself. Elise sniffed her. Alcide remembered how she had said that "her Henri" was gone, but it was clear the finality of this was devastating for her.

Seraphine hadn't yet made a sound. Not until the priest stepped forward, to attempt to comfort her, did she make any noise at all. Seraphine snarled at him, through clenched teeth. Father Benoit withdrew his outstretched hand. She snarled at him again.

Father Benoit took a couple steps back, until he was beside Alcide, and said, "She's stark, raving mad. It's too much for her."

"Olivier says that the filly has trapped her soul," Alcide said. If Seraphine heard him, she gave no sign. She was quieting, and slowly rocking. The two men walked away, and then stopped just outside the barn doors. It was still raining, and quite cold, but it was more like a mist.

"Do you think she might be possessed?" the priest asked.

"That is your field. She has been through more than a person can stand. If she comes back to us, she'll never be the same," Alcide said.

"Should we have someone from Hospice Vinatier come for her?" Father Benoit asked.

"What is that?" Alcide asked.

"The hospice, in Lyon, Hospice de la Charité. They renamed it, just this year," the priest said.

Alcide shuddered at the mention of the asylum. "You would lock her up in Lyon? They will inter her for years, decades, or maybe the rest of her life. People don't often come out of la Charité," he said.

"But she is snarling like an animal!" the priest said.

"She has hurt no one! She has not tried to hurt herself!" Alcide said.

"I see a recent injury on her face, largely healed, but it is from this season for sure," the priest said.

"She was struck by a horse," Alcide said.

"Ah, damage to her brain would account for some of this," the priest said.

"Her cheek was only bruised and cut," Alcide said. "She lost her child, she is obsessed with a foal, and then today you tell her she is a widow. We must give her a chance to recover, here, in familiar surroundings."

"Can she even take care of herself? She is unkempt," the priest asked.

"She's been working in a barn. Listen, she has cooked for me and herself every day, and she has slept soundly every night in her bed," Alcide said, wondering if lying to a priest was worse than ordinary lies.

"And you have not observed odd behavior until now?" the priest asked.

Alcide said, "What is odd? That which we are not used to seeing? I'm an old man who has been living without female company for many years. Most of what she does seems odd to me." He couldn't help but remember her nursing the foal, and struggled to put the image out of his mind.

Father Benoit looked into the barn, and then back at Alcide. "I am leaving this on you. If she harms herself, or anyone else, it will be on your hands, not mine," he said.

"I understand," Alcide said.

"If she needs to be protected in a place like le Vinatier, do the right thing and send for me right away," the priest said.

"I will," Alcide said.

Father Benoit nodded, wiped the rainwater from his face, looked into the barn once more, but left without reentering it. Once he was gone, Alcide went back in to check on Seraphine and the foal. She was singing Elise a lullaby while brushing her. Alcide left her there, and went to check on Bijou.

He found the large mare grazing. She seemed calm, and he scratched her near her withers. She was wet, but could have easily stepped out of the cold rain if she had wanted.

"What are we going to do, Bijou?" he asked, and she snorted. Alcide scanned in all directions, and saw fields and trees. No one was out in this, except for him and Bijou.

"Are you getting used to being alone? Horses prefer company," Alcide said.

Bijou shook her head, and Alcide smiled. He said, "Maybe not when they get older, eh?" He turned back toward the barn, and asked, "Do you want to come in? I will wipe you down, and put a wool blanket over you."

Bijou looked as if she were considering it for a moment, but then began to graze again. Alcide nodded, and went back into the barn.

27

◇◇◇◇◇

MONTAGNAT
1914

A letter from Henri

The next day, a letter arrived from the dead. It was from Henri, obviously written before he was killed. Alcide considered throwing it away, unread, but instead he read Henri's letter to himself, and never told Seraphine of its existence.

"Dear Seraphine,

My unit has bounded with another French unit in a race, against the Germans, toward the sea. We have joined up now with Belgian soldiers outside a Flemish town. Now we wait for orders to come. The race is over, we have run out of land, and simply attempting to maneuver around the enemy is no longer possible. We will have to fight directly, and while I hope this coming battle will be decisive in this war, I am not at all confident that I will see the end of it.

We met men coming off the line who were once members of a large unit, just as I am, and they were the few who were left. I hope only to give good account of myself, and I hope you will find peace.

I have always loved you, and I deeply regret that you and I did not amount to more, but the blame does not fall only to us. We cannot control the world around us, and some waste what good time they have in trying. You and I never did that. While our time, before my leaving, was far shorter than we had thought it might be, we made the most of it.

If I do not return, be certain that I will always be grateful to God for the time He gave me as your friend, your lover, and your husband.

Henri"

Alcide carefully folded the letter, and put it in his pocket. He would not show Seraphine, but he wondered if everyone should write a goodbye letter every so often. He thought that surely, if people wrote letters like this, as if they may die that day, everyone would be kinder and more appreciative with the people around them. No one would want their last word, or their last act, to be a cruel one. Alcide thought that those who dreamed of leaving defiant last words are people who have never been close enough to the time of their own last words.

He remembered his wife and Viola, and wondered what letter they might have written together, if they had known the letter would be found after they were lost. What if people sat down, each Sunday morning, and wrote a goodbye letter to the world with no intention of leaving it, but only to capture in writing who they themselves truly are, just in case?

Alcide looked around, and saw the barn, the fields, and the paddock. He nodded at the life he had chosen, of honest and hard labor, but there were times when he missed his books, and erudite friends, discussing lofty ideas.

The search for truth was different than simply facing reality. It was then that Bijou whinnied loudly. Not out of alarm, but only as a reminder. Alcide smiled again, and said, "*In equis, veritas.*" He thought that Bijou was telling him that her reality is her truth, and that this all goes on. Still, he thought that a routine of writing heartfelt goodbye letters, just in case the current week was a person's last week, might produce the best sort of prayers.

28

◇◇◇◇◇

MONTAGNAT
1914

Alcide was in the paddock with Bijou when he saw Seraphine leading Elise on a line. He had never seen her leading the foal outside of the barn, away from the paddock. They headed for the field. Neither seemed to care about the mud, but the foal was cautious being out and exposed.

They walked on, farther into the saturated field. It wasn't raining, but it wasn't sunny either. The air was cool, but worse, it was damp. Alcide thought they might walk as far as the baby's grave, and that perhaps Seraphine was planning to introduce Elise. They even turned in that direction for a few steps, but they suddenly reversed their course and headed back. He wondered which of them had made the decision.

Seraphine stumbled, but regained her feet without falling. It was then that Alcide first saw, and then heard, her talking to Elise. Speaking to a horse was not unusual. Alcide suspected horses had heard more human secrets than any other animal. What was odd was that Seraphine was responding to the horse, as if they were in a conversation.

"It is quite slick," Seraphine said.

Pause.

"Of course I remember that you warned me, but I felt like a walk," Seraphine said.

Pause.

"Well you needn't be haughty about it. I admitted you were right," Seraphine said.

Pause.

"Yes, you were," she said.

Pause.

"You were, don't deny it," Seraphine said.

Frowning, Alcide watched them approach, and decided that time would not make her who she had been. There was no healing this. She was in a different state. Just as hay cannot be replanted in the field, and once again turn green and lush, Seraphine had changed and could never again by as innocent and naïve as she once had been. She had transformed, not only in condition, but in purpose. Whatever destiny had been predicted, and guessed at, it was clearly not what was actually in the woman's future.

The young horse had mud to her cannons, and Seraphine's hem clung to her dirty shins.

"Oh well, let's drop the subject," Seraphine said to Elise.

This was who Seraphine was now, he thought. This wasn't a broken Seraphine. She was not in need of a cure, any more than a gargoyle was. Unsettling for some to see, perhaps, but she was as life had made her. Alcide felt sympathy for her, and empathy, but he also knew the changes were permanent.

29

◇◇◇◇◇

MONTAGNAT
1914

While Alcide was sweeping in the barn aisle, he heard Seraphine talking. While he could not see her, he had glimpsed her twenty minutes earlier, lying in a pile of hay in Elise's stall, with the foal standing a couple feet away.

Seraphine said, "A person has no idea of the risks, Elise. At the beginning, it seems that finding someone, and then marriage, children, and a life together are simply a matter of choices. Those things are supposed to naturally follow love and commitment. At the wedding, friends and family say only, 'Congratulations' and the like. What they all should be saying is 'Good luck' or 'May the Lord have mercy on you both' or something like that. Maybe the same as what someone might say when a friend is boarding a fragile boat in a storm."

She cleared her throat and said, "Oh, how rickety

the best marriage is, and how vulnerable the deepest love, when they set sail. If you fall in love with a person, you also fall in love with dreams. Just like sailors had thoughts of land, even as the storm worsened, and then to have them answered with jagged rocks that ripped the belly open, with death spilling out."

Alcide froze, and listened.

Seraphine continued, "To embrace a child for the first time, but whose arms did not move. No breath from tiny lips to be felt on my cheek. An infant who stirred within me, until the last day, but then born strangled, still and silent. A child who heard me inside my womb, but whose own voice would never sound outside of it. To go from enclosed in me to entombed in earth, without having taken a single breath of air, and without having seen the sun."

She said, "It was a fear I had pushed out of my mind, and a tragedy that happened to others. It not only came, but it arrived at what was supposed to be the most joyous moment. It wasn't just the loss of the child, but instead an agony at the exact moment that was meant to be so wonderful. To fall was one thing, to fall from a height was worse, and to plummet from the height of giving birth was like falling from Heaven."

Alcide heard her, and thought that maybe he should take her to the hospital in Lyon after all.

Seraphine said, "And then Esme, another mother, with baby born perfect and full of life, rejected her child physically and emotionally. She denied you care, food, protection, and love. She even attacked her baby, leaving you confused and alone! You were left with a permanent longing, even with me as a loving foster, even with never wanting your original mother back."

Seraphine said, "And to be both at once! To be the mother who fell from Heaven to the stones below, and then to try to fill the heart of the abandoned baby! It is too much!"

She gasped and then asked, "Or was it meant to be a mending? Of two pieces, shaped for others, but brought together? Once denied and thirsting, were you drawing from me, Elise, from a well that was overflowing? Or was I the destroyed well, and I only reminded of what might have been? Reminding you by having you drink from my broken edges?"

Alcide walked slowly to peer into the stall, and saw the Seraphine was in front of the foal, with her hands on Elise's face as she spoke.

Seraphine said, "Isn't it only natural that we came together? That our needs match us perfectly? Maybe my daughter left her ruined body and assumed yours?"

Alcide thought, *Even she is thinking of possession!*

"Or have I lost my mind? The way they looked at me. The priest made me afraid and angry. So much so, that I couldn't speak! The thoughts were clear in my head, words to say, but I couldn't form them. I wanted to hit him, and bite! He was talking to me as if he cared! He had no way to understand what I felt, and he looked at me as if I was insane. What would he have believed even if I could have gotten the words out? He was there when my baby slid from between my legs, and into death. He saw the blood, and the lifeless purple child, and his face only set hard. Not a word to me! Not a look! He simply walked out, as if I had failed somehow," she said.

Alcide saw her release the foal's face, and turn away. She said, "And why did the priest come here once again? To tell me that my Henri was at peace? How would the priest know the state of Henri's soul? My husband was called to war, his child died, and then I had nothing for him! He came home to the terror of this place, with horror in his own heart, he left, and his life was taken from him. Henri had no time to make peace with any of it, and I have no way to find peace."

"Maybe I *am* losing my mind, but am I alone?" she asked. "Esme went mad. We were bonded once, but then she took a set against me. She attacked her baby, and when I moved to save you, Elise, it was then that Esme hurt me. And Olivier, he let Esme loose; he was crazed. The wild boy, lives God knows where, and has been doing only the devil knows what. And he stole! He has the camera! He took it. And a photograph! He has me and you in that box. If Olivier won't give me the camera, he'll be sorry."

Elise took a step, and nickered.

"What is it?" Seraphine asked.

Alcide quietly stepped into view.

"How long have you been there?" Seraphine asked.

"I just now arrived," Alcide said.

Seraphine rolled her eyes, and said, "I have always talked to myself, you know. It is not a sign that I have gone mad."

"I believe you."

"Especially while I am working here in the barn," she said.

Alcide did not remember ever hearing her talk to herself before, and really, she had not been talking to herself, but instead to Elise. Still, there was no reason to argue with her.

"We should get Claire Voisine's camera back," she said.

It had been more than ten days since he had seen the boy, and despite the fact that the sun was beginning to set, he decided he would go to the cave. "I'll go," Alcide said.

She nodded, but said nothing more, and Alcide headed out.

30

◇◇◇◇◇

THE CAVE
1914

Olivier was in a dark corner of the cave, and sitting on a naturally formed stone shelf. He watched as Alcide came in, but it was clear that the old man could not see Olivier. Alcide walked over toward the pile of evergreen branches, and lifted a half-finished carving of a horse.

Olivier watched Alcide turn it in his hands, as if studying it, before putting it back where it had been. He resented Alcide brazenly walking in, and touching his things, but Olivier didn't say anything. The old man walked over to the wall, on another shelf, where all of Olivier's other carvings were.

Alcide picked up the figure of a man, and then of a horse. Olivier's face flushed hot, thinking Alcide's presence was such an invasion. Olivier saw him put those two carvings back, and then pick up two more—

this time a horse lying down, and a woman. And then the baby. Alcide stared at the wooden form of a human infant, and slowly put the other two back.

Olivier had carved all the others to the same scale; the man, woman, and horses were all correct when compared to each other, but the baby was three times larger. When Alcide examined between the carved baby's legs, Olivier knew that the old man saw that it was not a model of Seraphine's lost daughter.

He was grinding his teeth, watching Alcide, and he just wanted him to leave. The old man put the carving of the baby back on the shelf, and turned to leave, but it seemed something caught his eye.

"Not that," Olivier said to himself, and then he thought Alcide had heard him. The old man froze for a moment, but then he moved quickly, and picked up Claire's camera.

Damn, Olivier thought. *He's taking my camera.*

Alcide looked it over, and then turned and scanned the cave. Olivier froze, but he was furious. His hands were shaking with rage. *He came into my home and he is stealing!* he thought. He considered attacking the old man, and maybe brain him with a rock. *No*, Olivier thought. *He's old, but strong and wiry.* Olivier knew he'd have to be patient and go retrieve it from the farm, and next time, he would hide it better.

When Alcide began to walk toward the door of the cave, with the camera in his hands, Olivier did have one more flash of imagining getting the camera back. *Maybe in the woods, away from the cave*, he thought.

But then Olivier was alone once more. He sprang to his feet, paced twice, and then went out into the dark, trying to follow Alcide without being heard. *Everything used to work fine*, Olivier thought. *They lived on their farm, and I lived in here. Sometimes with bread and cheese, and even some eggs. Esme was okay, and Bijou. The woman was happy, and the man was happy. Even the goats seemed to be having fun, climbing on things. Everything was fine. Even when the man went to the war, even though she missed him, there was hope.*

"That foal," he said to himself in the dark, hearing the sounds of the old man ahead, somewhere in the woods. *That's when everything went bad. The woman's baby died, and then that demon that killed the baby, came into the foal, and made Esme and the woman insane. That broke the man's heart. With a broken heart in war, what chance does one have? It's all that wicked spirit in the foal; it's that fiend's fault.*

31

◇◇◇◇◇

PARIS
1922

Alcide sat across from me, took a deep breath, and told me more about that night. "As I walked back to the farm, through the dark forest, I held tight to that camera. I couldn't be sure, but more than once I thought I heard someone following me, and I suspected Olivier may have seen me coming out of his cave, carrying Claire's camera."

"But he didn't confront you," I said.

Alcide was quiet for a minute, and then said, "The woods smelled of autumn, but not the scent of cool air and colorful picnics. There was a different odor. The mid-November smell signifying that life was not returning, but instead ebbing. The scent of a trend toward death, or at least dormancy. No expectations, nor even surprises, of new shoots or blooms. The earth was tired, the trees fatalistic, and the air cooler each subsequent night.

There was just enough light to find my way, but not enough to feel safe while I did so, and the forest felt so resigned to the seasons that it was hard not to feel the same way. In the dark, there was the occasional sound of a twig snapping or the scuffling of feet in leaves, first to my right, then behind, then to my left. I suspected I was being followed by a broken boy, on my way to rejoin a broken woman, on a broken farm, bathed in sorrow and loss," Alcide said.

A question I'd had more than once, but had not asked, surfaced in my mind once more, and it seemed the best opportunity. "Why did you stay? Many men would have left. After all, you had agreed to help with managing a farm, not to somehow manage the human wreckage you had no idea was coming. Why didn't you bring her to the hospital? It might have even been better for her. What you were doing was well beyond what you had signed on for," I said.

Alcide stood once more and slowly walked around. "True, I had not expected all that had happened, but neither had the Arsenaults. It was not as if they tricked me into taking on more than I had wanted. I felt as if we had encountered all the hardship together, and while I was not an owner of the farm, it seemed to me that we were on the same team. You see? That my role was to take care of horses and goats, yes, but I felt Henri had entrusted the safety of his entire life to me, to keep all as well as possible until his return. While we all knew that he might not come home, although no one said those words, and it was obvious that his physical survival was at risk, we thought our task was simply to make sure his life was still there to return to, if he did not die. As it turned out, his life came apart while he still lived, and then he was killed," Alcide said.

"Do you think that fact increased the chances of his death at the front? Perhaps he didn't cling to life as hard, since the life he knew was no longer there in Montagnat?" I asked.

"Perhaps," Alcide said.

"So, if the truth had been kept from him, he might have lived," I said.

"People often get through arduous times by imagining returning home, and they even exaggerate to themselves about how wonderful returning will be. This can sometimes be part of the reason why a person returning home seems disappointed, because reality cannot match what someone built up in his mind. However, when the imagined homecoming fell apart for him, and reality proved to be even worse than he could have imagined, it may certainly have pulled the will out of Henri's body," Alcide said.

"And led to his death?" I asked.

"I'm sure it did not help his chances," Alcide said.

I hesitated, but then said, "So, you returned to the farm with the camera."

"I did," he said. "It wasn't the boy's to keep."

"It wasn't yours either," I said.

32

◇◇◇◇◇

MONTAGNAT
1914

Alcide carried the camera into the barn, and the moment Seraphine saw it, she asked, "You got it back."

Alcide said only, "It was in his cave, with some carvings."

She paused her brushing of Elise, and asked, "What carvings?"

"Quite remarkable wooden carvings of a man, a woman, horses, and a baby."

"My baby?" Seraphine asked, and she brushed more quickly.

"A baby boy. Maybe a carving of himself," Alcide said.

"You didn't see him?"

"I didn't, but he may have seen me," Alcide said, looking back, and out of the barn.

Seraphine stopped brushing for a moment and stared

at Elise's withers, before starting again. She said nothing.

"I need some sleep." Alcide said, and headed for the ladder to the loft.

"Are you taking that camera up there?" she asked.

He glanced down into the corner of Elise's stall, and saw that Seraphine's sleeping spot had become a bit more formal. There were arranged bales, and a few wool blankets with a small pillow. Alcide was glad for it, since it was mid-November after all, and the nights were quite cool. There had even been snow, although it was melted again by the cold rains they'd had since. He said, "Where else would I put it? No one lives in the house anymore."

"There is no need to say things like that," she said, and put down the brush.

Alcide said nothing else, climbed up, and walked over to his own sleeping space. He looked toward the house, and thought of how nice it would be to sleep in a proper bed, with a fire going, but then he lay down, with one hand on the camera, and fell asleep.

He woke to Seraphine's screams. Alcide dashed to the edge of the loft and, rubbing his eyes, looked down to see Olivier, with a filet knife in his hand, standing between Seraphine and Elise.

"You leave her alone! Come away from her!" Seraphine screamed.

"You don't understand! This horse is evil! Esme knew this foal was not right! She shunned it, and expected it to die!" Olivier said.

"She is not an 'it!' She is Elise, and I love her! She is innocent!" Seraphine said.

"It's some sort of demon, I tell you! Esme knew it! I am trying to free you! It took advantage of how sad you were when your baby died, and it came into this horse! Can't you see how it has taken over your life as well!" Olivier said. "I've got to kill it, and set you free!"

"Leave her alone! You're the evil one, if you could do such a thing!" Seraphine said.

Olivier began to slowly back closer to Elise, the knife held up to keep Seraphine back. "Maybe I am, my mother shunned me as well, and mothers must have a sense about these things. But I know this horse is a demon, I can feel it, and it has your soul twisted." Olivier was inching closer to Elise, who was pawing at the stall floor, wild-eyed.

Alcide began to climb down the ladder, slowly. He was off to one side of Olivier, and behind him. He knew he couldn't get to the boy easily, but he might get close enough to have a chance to help. However, Seraphine couldn't wait any longer. Olivier raised the knife, and took two more steps toward Elise. In a panic, Seraphine suddenly charged at Olivier, shrieking at the top of her lungs.

Without a doubt, Alcide knew, the boy could have stabbed her as they came together, but he did not. The two of them struggled, arms raised, her hands wrapped around Olivier's wrist with the knife held high in

Olivier's hand, both still standing. Alcide jumped the rest of the way down and rushed over. He ran at Olivier's back as the boy pushed Seraphine to the floor. Elise whinnied as Olivier stepped quickly to slash the foal's throat. Seraphine screamed at the top of her lungs, just as Alcide grabbed Olivier's arm.

The boy spun, and stabbed in a sweeping arc. Alcide didn't think the boy had any idea who had ahold of him, and the old man raised his left arm in defense. The blade plunged into Alcide's forearm, and he saw the tip come through as it passed between the bones.

Seraphine gasped, and lunged for Elise, hugging the horse around the neck, placing herself between Olivier and the filly. Olivier released the handle of the knife, with the blade remaining through Alcide's forearm. The old man never made a sound, he only doubled at the waist and held his left arm with his right hand.

"Oh my God, what have I done?" Olivier said, and he began to back away.

"Don't go," Alcide said. "This will mend. I know you didn't mean to. Stay, don't go." He was still bent at the waist, but he lifted his head enough to see Olivier, who was still moving toward the door.

Olivier said, "That demon made it happen!" and he pointed at Elise.

"Stop calling her that!" Seraphine said.

"It wasn't my fault! That horse is evil, and it's driving the woman mad!" Olivier said, and then he broke into a run and was gone.

Alcide looked at the knife, and the blood he was losing, which actually was not as much as he had expected. He looked over at Seraphine, as she comforted the horse. He said, "Seraphine, come here. Help me."

She came over, and Alcide said, "Grab the handle, and when I tell you to, you must pull it out quickly and as straight as you can."

Without hesitation, she grabbed it. Alcide said, "Alright, now when I say…"

Seraphine immediately yanked it out, and this time Alcide roared in pain. She turned, and started out after Olivier, with the knife in her hand.

"Where does he go?" she asked.

"Give me the knife," Alcide said.

"No! Where does he go? We can't wonder, each night, while we sleep if that little monster will return. Where does he go?" Seraphine asked.

"Leave the knife, and I'll tell you," Alcide said, wrapping a towel tightly around his injured arm.

"I'll find him myself!" she said, and began to leave.

"You'll never find it. It's too well hidden," Alcide said.

"Then tell me!" Seraphine said.

"Drop the knife, and I'll take you there," Alcide said.

Seraphine tossed the knife near Alcide's feet, and said, "I need you to stay here to keep Elise safe. So, now, I have no knife. Where does he go?"

"What will you do?"

"Where does he go?" she shouted, shaking, with a vein prominent on her neck.

"There is a cave, near the top of the ridge, where the tree line transitions," Alcide said.

"He lives alone in a cave?"

"He stays there. I'm not sure if that's the only place he stays. For all we know, he might not have even gone there. Also, he was prepared to kill the foal, and he did stab me. It's not quite dawn out there. What if he is hiding behind a tree, with a club? He would be able to kill you before you heard a sound," Alcide said.

"If he attacks me, and does not kill me in the first instant, anything I do to him will be considered defending myself, and we only need to show authorities you arm. He was going to kill Elise, and he drew blood from you. He's a maniac. I am going to end this," Seraphine said.

"He's the same boy you offered bread and cheese. He's the same Olivier that you had Henri follow out of concern for him. Just let him go," Alcide said.

"After what he did? He threatened to kill that baby!" Seraphine said, and pointed toward Elise.

Seraphine started to leave, when Alcide said, "He'll move on, after all this. Let him go. Why not just let him go? You'll never see him again."

Seraphine seemed to think about it for a second, but then she turned and was gone. Alcide picked up the knife, stuck it in a stall post. He went over, and checked the foal.

She seemed to be fine. He looked at the makeshift bandage around his arm. It would need proper cleaning, and then a doctor more than likely, although it was not bleeding through the dressing, and he could move his wrist and fingers. The pain, however, was substantial.

Alcide looked in the direction that Olivier and Seraphine had gone, sighed, closed the stall door, and went after them both, leaving the knife behind in the barn.

Once Alcide was climbing the wooded slope, he could hear Seraphine up ahead of him, although he couldn't see her. Alcide thought she would be making less noise if she were falling down the hill than she was making climbing it, which meant that Olivier would be fully aware that she was after him. Alcide knew that could prove to be dangerous, since the boy knew the slope well, and every step through the thick brush could have been into an ambush.

He continued up, not worrying about being silent, only about being quieter than Seraphine. Stumbling over a small, fallen log, Alcide landed on his injured arm. The pain shot into the small of his back, and then up and down his spine.

"Ugh," was all he said, but the noise ahead of him stopped. Seraphine had clearly frozen in place. Unable to see her in the pre-dawn shadows, he stayed still as well. His arm was throbbing, and he had a dull ache at the base of his skull, but he didn't move. Alcide focused on even trying to breathe silently, and then he heard her moving again.

He tried even harder to be silent, as he crept his way closer to the mouth of the cave.

33

◇◇◇◇◇

THE CAVE
1914

Olivier was in the same dark corner as he had been when Alcide retrieved the camera, although the cave was brightening because of the morning sun. He was trembling all over. He had never meant to hurt the old man. It was the evil, in that possessed filly, that made him do it.

Seraphine suddenly came through the doorway, and Olivier froze. She was looking in every direction. "Where are you?" she shouted.

Olivier said nothing. He sat still, and stared at her.

"I know you must be in here! Show yourself!"

Olivier couldn't think clearly. He'd stabbed the old man. *Is that why the woman came? Did the old man get weak from losing blood?*

"You stabbed Alcide!"

Not on purpose!

"You were going to kill Elise!"

If I had, you would be free right now! Olivier thought. He was still trembling, but any guilt he'd felt was changing into anger. *She's invading my home!*

Seraphine was stomping around, but not coming very far into the cave, and not really leaving the most brightly lit part near the mouth. Not until she spotted the carvings. She strode over, and picked up the man and woman.

"Is this me and Henri? Did you put a curse on us?" she demanded.

She doesn't know anything!

"You're the demon! You're the one who is evil! Come out!" she said.

"Get out!" Olivier screamed, and ran at her out of the dark corner. Seraphine did not run away, but instead charged right back at him. They collided with such force, the air came out of them both, and they went to the ground. Still, their arms were flailing and grabbing at each other's clothing, hair, and skin.

"You're a monster. Your mother shunned you, and I see why!" Seraphine said.

"All babies are monsters! Maybe me and the foal and your dead baby, too!" Olivier said.

"Shut up! Elise is pure! She is the only pure one around here!" Seraphine said.

Olivier landed a solid punch to her mouth, and blood ran from her lip. She let him go, and grabbed her chin.

Olivier jumped up, and began to run toward the mouth of the cave, but then she tackled him from behind.

"I won't let you go kill her!" she said, and grabbing his hair on the back of his head, drove his face into the cave floor.

Olivier lay motionless under her weight, until he felt it shift. He twisted beneath her, driving his elbow into her ear. She cried out and fell off, and Olivier rose to his feet. She got to her knees, and he kicked her in the ribs. She fell again, this time on all fours. Olivier watched her, unsure of what to do, both of them breathing hard. She slowly stood, turned to face him, and then suddenly threw a flurry of awkward punches. One landed on the side of his jaw, and the other struck him in the neck. Seraphine turned and ran, but only deeper into the cave. He chased, dove, and grabbed her ankles together. Seraphine screamed and fell.

She immediately twisted around, and struck him in the side of the head with his half-finished carving of Esme. Olivier saw a flash, and the pain was awful. He tried to get his feet under him, but he wobbled, and then fell against her as she rushed at him again. They both went to the floor, clutching at each other, biting, scratching, and punching. Olivier was sure if he didn't kill her, that she would kill him. His vision was not yet even clear, but he fought with everything he had.

34

◇◇◇◇◇

PARIS
1922

"By the time I reached the mouth of the cave," Alcide said to me, "my arm was throbbing, and although I couldn't see much blood, I was a bit weak. Maybe it was simply coming to grips with the knowledge that a knife had run through my arm."

"Certainly understandable," I said.

"When I entered, Seraphine and Olivier were in a deathmatch. It was clear it wasn't a fight to convince the other that he or she was wrong, or to force the other to go away. It was a fight to the death," Alcide said.

"How could you tell? She hadn't brought the knife," I asked.

"They already had marks and scratches on their faces and arms when I arrived, and I stepped into the cave in time to see Olivier run straight at Seraphine. Just as he ran her into the floor of the cave, she struck him with a piece of wood he had been carving," Alcide said.

"Good lord," I said.

"Despite my shouts to stop, they rolled on the ground, while punching, clawing and biting each other, until Olivier found himself on top, straddling her waist, and he grabbed a rock the size of a small melon. This he lifted over his head, with both hands, intending to smash her head with it," Alcide said.

"So, at that point, he did intend to kill Seraphine!" I said.

"I rushed forward and, with my one good arm, grabbed his. The rock fell out of his grasp, and onto the top of his own head. Olivier immediately fell off her and onto the floor," Alcide said.

"Dead?"

"He would've died, had I not stopped Seraphine, who went for the same rock intending to hit Olivier with it, again, and finish him off," Alcide said.

"How did you stop her?"

"I stepped between them, and she was exhausted. She tried to push through me, but couldn't," Alcide said.

"What did Olivier do?" I asked.

"It was then that Olivier stumbled to his feet, as blood ran down his left cheek, and he went out of the cave."

"And Seraphine?" I asked.

"No sooner had Olivier fled, then she fell over. I helped her to her feet, she was semiconscious, and I got her out of there. Managing as best I could with one arm, it was difficult going, until out of nowhere, Suzanne, the neighbor girl appeared and, without a sound, took one of Seraphine's arms around her shoulders. I did the same with the other. We got her to the barn, and Suzanne promptly left," Alcide said.

"Had she been in the woods? Had she followed Olivier, Seraphine, or you to the cave?" I asked.

"I haven't any idea," Alcide said. "Seraphine and I were alone with the animals, and I slept in the stall with Seraphine and Elise that night."

"Did Olivier return?" I asked.

"The next morning, it was Claire who arrived. I suppose Suzanne communicated something was wrong, or perhaps she brought her mother, without explanation, and without coming into the barn," Alcide said.

"What were Seraphine's injuries?" I asked.

"Bruises and scratches, and a large bump on her head. The pain was enough that she was nauseous," Alcide said. "Claire tended to us both, after going to the house for supplies. She told me I'd need to see a doctor for my arm, and I agreed, but I never did go."

"And did Olivier get medical attention?" I asked.

Alcide stared at the floor for a long time, and then said, "I have no idea."

I didn't say anything for a moment, and then I asked, "By the way, when did you give the camera back to Claire?"

35

◇◇◇◇◇

MONTAGNAT
1914

Alcide's arm was in a sling as he brushed Bijou. It had rained the entire previous day, and it was still falling in sheets outside. He had figured out how to tend and milk the goats, and care for the chickens, all with one arm. Seraphine, of course, took care of Elise.

While they were both healing, and working within sight of each other, not much was being said. As the sun was setting that day, Alcide saw that much of the level ground outside the barn held standing water, and the rain had not slowed. He thought that surely the stream had overflowed its banks.

Shortly, after dark, he heard the first distant rumble. Another thunderstorm was on the way. It was so odd, he thought, that so many storms had come through, and in mid-November. There should have been more snow than rain at that time of year, but the day had been weirdly warm, and even the rain wasn't as cold as it should be. It smelled like hay growing older, and with electricity in the air. Even Bijou, usually calm, was restless.

"There's a storm coming," Seraphine said to the entire barn, and to no one.

"The chickens and goats are all in for the night," Alcide said.

He took Bijou off the crossties, and led her into her stall. It was then that Elise became upset. She whinnied, snorted, and scratched at the floor.

Seraphine kept saying, "Everything is fine, everything is fine" but it wasn't. Elise became more and more agitated.

Alcide went to the stall, and said, "Let me help you."

Elise kicked the wall.

"Stop! Stop!" Seraphine said, and then there was a deafening clap of thunder that seemed to be directly overhead. Elise only became worse. Alcide got to the stall, and had just opened the door, when Elise charged directly at him. Alcide was knocked down, catching himself on his one, good arm, and Elise ran straight out of the barn, and into the storm, just as there was another brilliant flash of lightning and a then an equally loud peal of thunder.

"Elise!" Seraphine screamed, and chased after her.

Alcide slowly got to his feet. There was another flash of lightning, and as Alcide walked slowly and painfully to the door, the thunder crashed again. Coming out into the dark and the rain, he scanned for them as his eyes adjusted. In the next flash, he saw them heading into the field, which looked more like a shallow lake. Alcide walked as fast as he could, following them, but he knew he'd never catch up. The next clap of thunder was so loud, he reflexively ducked at the sound.

Scanning again as he reached the edge of the field, the mud beneath the standing water was ankle deep. There was another flash, and Alcide said only, "Jesus," but he didn't see either of them. The thunder seemed to slam into the ground, as if it were the palm of the hand of God, trying to flatten everything.

The smell of mud filled his nose, as he blinked at the drops striking his face, and the water on the ground seemed warmer than the rain that was falling.

Alcide then heard shrieking, in the dark, and while straining to see, another flash of lightning lit up the world. A figure not that far ahead, arms stretched to the sky, screaming unintelligibly. A wail of utter passion and despair. He thought it must be Suzanne again, the girl who raged at storms, or maybe she summoned, and then celebrated, them. Thunder drowned out her screams, as Alcide hurried to close the distance.

It was not Suzanne. Alcide realized as he approached that it was Seraphine, and she was standing over the gravesite of her stillborn daughter. In the next flash, he saw that the flood had raised the simple, wooden casket to the surface of the mud. Seraphine stumbled a few steps away, fell to her knees, and screamed again, just as before except not at the sky, but at the Earth itself.

When Alcide got to the casket, he could just make out the sight of the casket's lid broken open, and it staggered him as well.

With the next flash, Alcide saw the baby's face. Eyeless, skin beginning to turn black, lips pulled back, and tiny teeth revealed.

Alcide looked over at Seraphine, and said, "Come back with me to the barn!"

There was thunder; the time between flashes of light and crashes of sound were shortening, with the storm seemingly directly above them now.

Another flash of lightning, and still the driving rain. The thunder swallowed her first words, but then Alcide heard her say, "I was never meant to see those teeth! They were hidden inside the gums!" She screamed again, but it became a deep howl of agony, and Alcide felt a shiver down his spine at the sound of her pure anguish.

"Come back with me, Seraphine! Before we are struck! We will look for Elise together in the morning!" Alcide said.

Just then, Elise, some distance away and barely audible, whinnied in the dark, and a flash of lightning revealed her.

"Oh God! She's there!" Seraphine said.

"Don't go!"

Seraphine struggled to her feet and went toward

where they had seen Elise. Alcide began to follow, but tripped, as if over the next clap of thunder, and fell on his injured arm in the deep mud. He nearly passed out from the pain, covered in muck, with it in his mouth and eyes, he fought to sit up. When the lightning next flashed, he couldn't see where they had gone.

Alcide's energy was spent, and he was in agony. He was tempted to lie down, and just give up. Alcide thought, *why am I here? What am I doing here? A man of my age—this is all for a younger man. To bear witness? To be killed?*

As the next clap of thunder faded, he thought he heard Seraphine scream one more time. Alcide took a deep breath, steeled himself, and drew on whatever reserves he had left. He crawled to the dead baby and, with his one good arm, placed the broken pieces of the casket lid over her. He looked back toward the barn, and honestly thought it might be too far for him to make it, but he fought to stand. In the next flash, he glanced once more for any sign of Seraphine or Elise. Seeing none, and with the thunder just a touch less intense, and perhaps more distant this time, he slowly staggered his way back to the barn, the rain rinsing the mud from his face, ears, and neck.

Once back inside, he went into Elise's stall, and sat in the dry hay. Bijou whinnied from a few stalls away.

"I don't know, Bijou."

He tried to take some clothes off, but his injured arm

hurt too badly. He lay down, pulled a wool blanket over himself, and said, "If I wake up, I wake up. If not, so be it. *Fiat voluntas tua homini.*"

Alcide stared at the ceiling of the barn. His limbs became heavier, and his field of vision shrank. It became darker and the next thunder sounded muted.

He then heard the voice of his daughter, Viola. She said only, "Rest, Papa."

Alcide inhaled deeply, for what felt like a full minute of drawing in air. His chest inflated, painfully and fully, and then that air slowly drained out of him. It felt as if a rope was being pulled from his chest, and out through his mouth.

He wondered if he was dying, and then he fell asleep.

36

◇◇◇◇◇

THE CAVE
1914

Olivier had returned to the cave. He knew he was alone in there, but he kept checking the entrance anyway. He had spent the storm, sitting up, waiting for the bleeding to stop, but the rain ended first. The pain was excruciating. He had tried to stay awake in case anyone came after him, but, dizzy and weak, he had fallen asleep in spite of himself. When he woke, he was parched, and went out to drink all the water in the catch-bucket. After that, Olivier knew what he had to do.

He returned inside and shoved his clothes into his bag, with his head still pounding. Every few minutes, he would stop, and put his hand over his left ear, close his eyes, and wait for the pain to subside.

"I'll head east, that's where. East out of here, and away from this," Olivier said.

He chose his favorite carving of a horse, a man, a

woman, and the oversized carving of the baby. These he put in the bag with the clothing, and tied it closed.

Olivier placed the remaining wooden figures deep in the cave, on top of a pile of dry kindling and a few pieces of wood. Walking to the entrance, he carefully put his bag down, and then went back to light the fire. In no time, he saw the flames from the kindling were blackening the wood and the carvings above them. He was bent at the waist, trying to stay below the smoke, but soon he couldn't get low enough, and he quickly left the cave, snatching up his bag on the way out. Smoke came out also, rising from the mouth of it, and heading skywards towards the clouds.

He swung the bag over his right shoulder, and even that move made his headache worse. Olivier could feel his heartbeat from his cheekbone, along the side of his face, and up over his ear. *That rock got me good*, he thought. He did not blame Alcide. In fact, Olivier thought Alcide had likely saved his immortal soul.

"Thou shall not kill," Olivier said. The smoke filled almost the entire entrance now, as if a giant chimney had fallen over. *That demon almost got me to damn myself. If I had killed the woman, I would be destined for the flames*, he thought. He wanted nothing more than to get away from all of that.

Of course, on his way, he'd steal Esme back from the old man he sold her to. He'd gone to check on her, now and then, and she had actually put on a little weight.

She had no business pulling the old man's rickety cart, though, and the man gave Olivier so little money for her, it was only fair that he would take her back, he thought. He and Esme would go, and start anew. It was a cold time of year to strike out—it was late in the year—but he would find a way. He always did.

Olivier tried to peer into the smoke, but could not even see the flames any longer, and so he turned away. He winced with the headache again, but slowly walked on, knowing the smoke might bring someone. *It had been a good cave*, he thought. He wished he had a little more cheese.

37

◇◇◇◇◇

SMALL FARM
JUST OUTSIDE
BOURG-EN-BRESSE
1914

Olivier stood, holding a weathered rope halter in his hands. Looking at the little walkout where Esme was, he found it sad that she had once had a lovely stall, inside a barn, that was kept clean. At the Arsenault's, Esme also had a paddock, and a meadow to share with Bijou. That was back before that twisted foal had come, and before all of their lives had been turned upside down.

Here, the walkout Esme was standing in had only three rickety walls and a roof, and the structure was surrounded by mud. A hay bag hung limply on a pole.

As the sun was setting, he was already quite chilled, and Olivier didn't want to wait any longer. His headache did not hurt as badly, but he felt as if his thoughts were a bit foggy. He carefully came out of the bushes and walked slowly toward the fence. Esme nickered.

"Quiet, girl," Olivier whispered. He passed through the rails of the fence and went to the walkout. It was barely large enough for Esme to turn around inside of it. Olivier looked around the property, to the small shed, and over to the house. Unable to see where the cart was, he decided it must be behind one of the structures. However, all of the tack was hanging in Esme's space. The bridle, bit, reins, and harness were all there. He would not take any of those, however. *Those belong to Monsieur Terreaux, the old man, and after all, I'm not a thief*, Olivier thought. He slipped the halter onto Esme, and gently coaxed her out of the walkout. He looked over at the gate, and winced at how much closer to the house it seemed now.

He checked the house windows, but no lights had come on yet. Olivier saw no movement, and heard nothing coming from that direction. He straightened and began leading Esme that way. She walked with her head down, ears relaxed, as if resolved to whatever the outcome would be. Opening the gate, he led her through, and turned her around while closing it.

From this new angle, he spotted the cart behind the shed. "No more of that," he whispered to Esme, and headed for the dirt road.

Just as her front hooves reached it, a voice called out, "Thief!"

Esme turned only her head, and Olivier looked around her, to see old man Terreaux coming. He knew that, if he wanted to, he and Esme could simply outrun the man, but he waited.

"You are a thief!"

"She needs to leave here," Olivier said.

"What will I do? I can't pull the cart by myself."

"What do you use the cart for?" Olivier asked.

"When I have to move heavy loads of course."

Olivier looked at Esme, patted her nose. It was cold, and there was still enough light to see her breath mix with his own. "What loads?"

The old man looked back at the cart, and then at Esme, and said, "Could be almost anything."

"I'm sorry, Monsieur, but I have to take her back," Olivier said.

"Even if I let you, Olivier, you must return my money," he said.

"I think it was a fair amount, for how long you have had her. *Je ne l'ai pas vendue. Je vous l'ai simplement louée*," Olivier said.

"Leased? You never mentioned that it was merely a lease," he said.

Olivier turned, and began to lead her away. Old man Terreaux moved to stop him, and asked, "Why did you sell her, when now you need her?"

"I was living in the wild, and could not care for her. In the barn where she was, she rejected her foal. The foal is evil, and it has even taken over the mind of a widow. An old farmhand was going to kill this horse, so I ran the mare off to save her life. When I later collected her, all I had to eat for myself was a bit of bread, and nothing for her. We are in early winter now, and I knew I couldn't care for her properly, so I brought her to you," Olivier said. "Now, I am taking her back."

"So, she was technically stolen already," he said.

Olivier sighed, and said, "I wish I could give you all your money back. I have some."

"Where will you take her?"

"East. And I will find work, in a barn that will take us both. A cave is not enough anymore, because I have someone to take care of."

Olivier saw that when Terreaux looked him over, his shoulders fell, and he said, "Why don't we go inside?"

"I am taking her," Olivier said.

"I understand, but you don't need to walk off into the dark and the cold right this moment. Come inside, and I will share some soup with you. You can sleep near the fireplace, and then go with the mare in peace."

Olivier felt apprehension well up inside him. *Would the old man poison me to keep the horse, and bury my body away from the house? Who would ever know?*

"You suddenly have decided to let her go?" Olivier said.

"I'm old. I will move fewer heavy loads, and the horse will have a better life. You are quite devoted to her; first you saved her life, and then to try to steal her like this, so in the morning take her east. For tonight, come eat and sleep properly."

With Esme tied outside, they entered the dark house together. Terreaux lit an oil lamp, and immediately went to the large fieldstone fireplace, and started a fire. It was crackling in no time, and the room warmed quickly.

There was a wooden table with three chairs, a simple stove, and an icebox perched upon four legs. Terreaux walked past it, however, and outside through a door beside it. Returning with a pot, he placed it on the stove and came back to where Olivier was standing.

"Please sit," Terreaux said, motioned to a chair, and took the one beside it.

Olivier sat, and then asked, "Have you lived here long?" The fenced area around the walkout was nothing but mud, and before it had gotten very dark, Olivier had not seen a single thing a man would have intentionally planted.

"For quite some time, yes," the old man said.

"What is it you do here?" Olivier asked. Just then, the pot's lid on the stove began to clatter softly.

"Pardon me," he said. Terreaux rose, went to the stove, and ladled soup into small bowls. He put a spoon in each, and then, using his fingers, pinched a wad of butter off a plate and dropped it into one of the bowls. He did the same for the second bowl. Carrying both, he returned to the table, and placed one in each spot.

He then sucked the butter off his fingers.

Olivier slowly stirred his until the butter was a melted streak on top of the opaque soup. Tasting it, he asked, "Carrot?"

"And garlic," Terreaux said, "Olivier, what if you don't find a farm east of here? The crops are in, some of the animals will be sold or butchered so farms won't need help like they will in the spring, even with the young men gone to fight."

"I will find something," Oliver said.

"But what if you don't?"

Olivier looked at Terreaux's bowl, and asked, "Are you going to eat?"

Terreaux looked at his bowl, but didn't immediately pick up his spoon.

I have been poisoned, Olivier thought, but then the old man had some.

"I have to find something. Hopefully, some place without evil," Olivier said, and took another bite. The soup was actually quite tasty.

Terreaux leaned over, and whispered, "There is no evil here."

"What do you mean?" Olivier asked.

"Stay here. Why not?"

"Monsieur, I am sorry, but you have nothing for me to do. A paddock of mud and a field overgrown with weeds. No livestock at all. To be honest, and I certainly appreciate your generosity all the more because of it, but I am not sure how you will make it through the winter yourself," Olivier said.

Terreaux stood up, and walked around the table. "I do have some money."

Olivier took another spoonful of soup into his mouth. It had been some time since he was able to eat anything like it. Terreaux came around behind Olivier, and the boy froze.

The old man said, "Stay here with me. You don't have to be alone all the time."

Olivier swallowed.

"You don't have to be alone, and I don't have to be alone."

Olivier felt Terreaux's hands on his shoulders, and then they started rubbing. He couldn't move, except to look down as the wrinkled hands slid down the front of Olivier's chest, and it was then he found the ability to jump out of the chair, spilling his soup, and moving away from Terreaux.

"Stay back!" Olivier said.

"But if you leave with the mare, I'll be all alone."

"Stay away from me," Olivier said, backing up.

"I could be very nice to you. And you could have soup," he said, and motioned toward the upturned bowl.

"I'm leaving right now," Olivier said, cautiously walking sideways toward the door.

"But you can't go. Don't leave me here, completely by myself," Terreaux said, his facial expression was one of deep sadness.

Oliver said, "I am going." He pushed the door open, and stepped into the cold, dark evening. The only light coming out through the window. He walked over to Esme, untied her, and began to walk quickly toward the road until he heard the door open behind him, and the cocking of a rifle.

Olivier looked back, and standing just outside the door was Terreaux, aiming an old Gras rifle at him and Esme.

"You are staying here," Terreaux said. "We can be nice to each other, and I can teach you things. We will not be alone anymore."

Olivier could see his aim was not steady. "Monsieur Terreaux, that rifle has a single shot. When was the last time it was fired? The cartridge is very old, I'm sure. If you try to kill this horse, and I hear you pull the trigger, but the cartridge does not fire, I will run to you and beat you to death."

"Maybe death would be better," Terreaux said, but did not lower the rifle.

"Your aim is terrible. It's dark. Even if you do fire that rifle, and you miss me, I will run to you and beat you, and perhaps leave you badly beaten and alive," Olivier said.

"You said you would kill me," Terreaux said, his voice breaking, his aim becoming even less stable.

"If you harm this horse, or even try to, I will break your back and leave you," Olivier said.

For a moment, they stood there, and then Terreaux

lowered the rifle. He began to sob as he sat down where he was. Olivier walked quickly, leading Esme onto the road, and heading east. He could barely make out the road.

"I am sorry, Esme, I know it's cold. Tomorrow, we will find a new place," Olivier said.

Esme startled at the sound of a rifle shot behind them, but Olivier did not.

"We'll find a safe, warm place with nice hay for you," he said.

38
◇◇◇◇◇
PARIS
1922

Alcide said, "Yes, Robert, I said that. I went into Elise's stall, and simply sat in the dry hay. Couldn't even take off my wet clothing because my arm hurt so badly. I lay down, pulled a wool blanket over myself, and said, 'If I wake up, I wake up. If not, so be it.' And I meant it."

"That's not all you said. You spoke Latin, basically saying 'God's will be done.' You did go to seminary, didn't you? It's more than a simple classical education," I said.

"Focus on the story, and not my CV. Obviously, I'm telling you a story, and I am not applying for employment," Alcide said.

I leaned forward in my chair, and said, "Fine, you woke up in the barn. You didn't succumb. It wasn't your time. You must have been absolutely frozen, though, in those wet clothes."

"When I awoke, I was cold, yes, and I'm not quite sure how I might have managed if the priest, Father Benoit, hadn't come," Alcide said.

"How did the priest know to go?" I asked.

"Claire told him that things at the farm had gotten violent. He had come to see if he could convince me that Seraphine needed to go to the asylum, to le Vinatier," Alcide said.

"Had she returned by the time the priest got there?"

"She had not. I asked the priest if he'd seen her, or the filly, and he said there was no sign of them," he said.

"But the priest helped you?" I asked.

"He went up into the loft, retrieved dry clothes for me, and then he helped me change into them. He checked my arm, and cleaned it. He said the wound was filthy."

"You had fallen in the mud onto it," I said.

"That's right. The priest cleaned it, and put a new dressing on it," Alcide said.

"He did not seem that caring before. Seraphine thought he was cold," I said.

"Perhaps women and babies made him uncomfortable. Not that he was warm with me, either, but he did help me. He even offered to take me into the house and start a fire," Alcide said.

"Did you go into the house?"

Alcide said. "I wanted to check on the animals, after that storm the night before, I was quite concerned. I especially wanted to check on Bijou."

"What about after? Surely a warm fire would've been nice," I said.

"I might have, but it did not work out that way," Alcide said.

"I see. Did you consider going to check on Olivier? Or was he more of a danger than a concern by then?" I asked.

"I wanted the boy to disappear. I wished Olivier would slip away, and even though he stabbed me, I hoped he was not too badly hurt," Alcide said, "Plus, I was still weak, and I had enough to do."

"Why? Why do? You should have simply left the farm," I said, "It wasn't yours after all. At that point, you were down two horses, the man and woman of the homestead were gone, and a young farmhand had stabbed you, and no one knew if he was still lurking about."

"That's just what the priest said to me," Alcide said, rubbing his left forearm.

"And you were hurt besides," I said.

"I was," Alcide said.

"Then why stay?"

Alcide looked all around, and then at his hands, and then said only, "It wasn't over yet."

"What?"

"It. Whatever *it* was, I could feel that it wasn't over yet," Alcide said.

"How long did the priest stay with you?" I asked.

"Long enough so that we, together, went out and

reburied Seraphine's baby properly. While there was some standing water in the field, the gravesite was soft mud. The priest spoke prayers again, and this time the prayers were simple words without performance. With no Earthly audience but me, he spoke to God, the Holy Virgin, and to Jesus, and the priest seemed to give little thought this time about how he looked or sounded while doing it," Alcide said.

"And then?"

"We buried the little casket, placing the largest stones upon it first, and then the soil," Alcide said.

"And once that was done?" I asked.

"The priest left."

I got up, and walked across the terrace. Looking down toward the canal, at Bassin de l'Arsenal, I asked, "He simply left?"

"We had finished. He was not going to work in the barn. We were not friends. The priest told me to tell Seraphine, if she returned, that he must talk to her," Alcide said.

"Did you ever see Seraphine again?" I asked.

Alcide sighed, and then said, "She came back a few hours later. After I tended the goats, when I might have thought of starting that fire in the house fireplace, I saw Seraphine in the distance, walking side by side with Elise, ever so slowly, toward the barn. She was a fright, just as I had been. Soaked, exhausted, and covered in mud. The filly was the same."

"And you helped her, just as the priest had helped you."

"Certainly not!" Alcide said.

"Why not?"

"I would not undress and dress her. She would have to do that herself, and besides, she had the use of both arms," he said.

I rolled my eyes. Of course, I hadn't meant removing her clothes. "I wasn't asking that. I only wondered if you helped her. Did you make her a fire inside the house?"

"She didn't say a word to me as she and the filly walked by. She only held up a hand, to have me to wait outside the barn, and they both went in. Not long after, I heard her call my name."

39

◇◇◇◇◇

MONTAGNAT
1914

Alcide went into the barn, and found Seraphine, with her face and neck washed, her body wrapped in blankets, and laying on her hay bed in Elise's stall. The filly, however, was still soaked and filthy.

In the softest voice, Seraphine said, "Alcide, Alcide. Please see to her? I would, but I haven't the strength, no strength."

"How are you? Are you warming?" Alcide asked.

"Warming warm, yes-yes. Please, s-see to her and bring her back to me-me in here, yes?" she said.

Alcide looked hard at the woman, as her eyes closed. The filly, he could see, was shivering. He put a lead rope on Elise, and led her a short distance away from the stall. There, he used an old moth-eaten blanket to try to mop up some of the water off the animal, and wipe some of the wet mud off. He would brush off the rest of the mud once it dried, he thought, but he wanted to immediately get the horse as dry as possible.

Behind him, Bijou whinnied loudly as she watched, as if giving advice.

"I know," he said. Once the old blanket was just about saturated, he pulled it off, and laid it over a wooden rail. Next, Alcide took a fine, thick woolen blanket and threw it over her, covering her from her withers to her tail. The filly was silent, and perfectly still. Alcide wiped her head with a towel, and hung that as well. Bijou snorted her approval, and he led Elise back to the stall where Seraphine was sleeping. Alcide took the rope lead off the filly, stepped out of the stall, and closed the gate behind him.

"Man, man," Seraphine said.

"I thought you were sleeping," he said.

"I am-am-am."

Alcide thought her voice sounded like an adult, mimicking a little child's voice. "What is it?" he asked.

"We we will be leaving the farm," she said.

"Where will we go? What about the animals?" Alcide asked.

Her voice became even more soft and childlike, loaded with fatigue, and she said, "Not you. Elise and I will be leaving. You can have the farm-farm-farm with all the animals."

He thought she must have lost all of her senses. "You get some sleep," Alcide said.

"Sleep-sleep, yes, but we will leave-leave-leave," Seraphine said.

Alcide said nothing more, and her breathing slowed and deepened.

Days later, the filly Elise, not even 200 kilograms herself yet, carried two packs on her back, and was tied to the outside of the paddock fence. Seraphine was cleaner and better dressed than Alcide had seen her in the last two months.

"It's not good for that horse to carry too much weight so young. You'll bend her," Alcide said.

"I'll rest her, rest her, and take it off when I do. We are in no hurry to get-get-get anywhere," she said.

"You don't have enough water," Alcide said.

"We will find some along the way," Seraphine said, "Find some."

Alcide tilted his head and said, "Please, just stay here. At least until spring. The nights are cold, and will get colder."

She pointed at the horse and said, "Blankets, blankets, blankets."

"The priest said he needs to talk to you," Alcide said.

Seraphine suddenly became very still, and she lowered her head. Looking up through her bangs, she spoke in a suddenly deeper voice, and said, "He can go to Hell."

Alcide sighed, and said, "I could come with you. To help."

Seraphine's entire body language relaxed, she stepped forward, put her hand on Alcide's cheek and said, "Sweet you, sweet you." She lowered her hand, and smiled.

Alcide almost suggested she leave the horse, Elise, behind, but he knew she never would.

"Goodbye," she said. She waved at the barn and the paddock, and said, "Goodbye, Bijou, bye goats, bye-bye chickens. Bye-bye-bye."

"Seraphine, you can always come back. And I'll make you a hot dinner, and build a fire. You can come back in the middle of the night. Anytime you'd like. It's your farm," Alcide said.

"Papers are on the table. It's your farm now, Alcide-cide. Bye-bye," she said as she led the horse away.

"Good luck, Seraphine," Alcide said.

"Goodbye, goodbye, goodbye, Henri, Henri," she said, looking out at the field, "Goodbye, *mon bébé*. Henri, *bébé*, Henri, *bébé*. *Adieu, à Dieu, à Dieu*."

Alcide watched her slowly head down the road, Elise beside her. The horse looked relaxed, and as she walked away, Seraphine ran one hand through her hair.

40

◇◇◇◇◇

PARIS
1922

I sat there, and folded my arms. "She walked away."

"That is what happened. She led her Elise down the road," Alcide said.

"And you never saw them again," I said.

"That is correct," Alcide said. "I stayed on the farm for a while. It was quiet and lonely. There was more milk than I could drink or sell, and the same with the eggs. Bijou was still there, but she became quieter, and lazier."

"Was it difficult to manage it by yourself?" I asked.

"The work was the best part, but eventually, I was giving eggs and milk away, and this was harming other farms in the area. I began to sell the goats and chickens, which only gave me less work, and more idle time. Like Bijou, I was getting bored," Alcide said.

"But you like farm work," I said.

"I wasn't ready for the unending cycle of the same

day, lived again and again, and doing that until I died. Especially not there, because although I owned it, it wasn't really my place. I had the deed, but it was unnatural. Living out my years there would have been the same as a sailor, marooned on a remote island, losing track of the days. Doing repetitive tasks, existing on nostalgia, until, surprised, he came to his last day," Alcide said.

"So, you decided to sell the farm?" I asked.

"I didn't. I was too trapped in the cycle to decide to do that. It was when Jean and Claire Voisine came to the farm," Alcide said.

"Jean Voisine was back from the war?" I asked. "How long were you there alone? Years?"

"Just a little more than one year, but he had been wounded, and was sent home. Luckily for a farmer, it wasn't his legs, arms, or back," Alcide said.

"Did you know he was back before they came to you? Had you seen him?" I asked.

"The postman came by a couple days before and asked if I had seen Voisine yet. I said I had not even known he was home," Alcide said.

"So, the Voisines simply came to your farm. Just them?" I asked.

"It was only Jean and Claire," he said.

41

◇◇◇◇◇

MONTAGNAT
1916

Alcide came walking out of the house as Claire Voisine came walking off the road with a man who wore a patch over his left eye.

"Madame Voisine, nice to see you," Alcide said.

"Monsieur Chrétien, this is my husband, Jean," Claire said.

Alcide shook his hand, and could see dark, fresh scars tracing out from beneath the patch. "Nice to meet you."

"And you," Jean said.

"How has your return been?" Alcide said.

They looked at each other, and then Claire said, "We heard that you have been selling your goats."

To Alcide, Claire seemed sad. He doubted it was about the goats, and said, "I have sold some. About half of them. I sold some chickens, too."

"Monsieur, would you be willing to sell us the entire

farm, including the animals?" Jean asked.

"Please, call me Alcide," he said. "Why would you want it? I cannot find a market for all this place produces. Even with three of you, you would have extra, not to mention the animals you have already."

"I am attracted by the land, to be honest. It gets more water, and is richer, than the land we already own," Jean said.

The land. This land, Alcide thought. He remembered those who thought the land might be troubled. *Energy lines.*

"Will you keep your land?" Alcide asked.

"We are not interested in a trade," Claire said.

"That wasn't what I was asking. I was only curious if you would keep both," Alcide said.

"We intend to keep both, but perhaps move into this house. It is in better shape, and since it seems our daughter will never leave our home, the additional space would be nice," Jean said.

"Would you be willing to sell it? Of course, you may take your time to consider it," Claire said.

"I have no idea what a fair price would be," Alcide said, and then he couldn't help but look at Jean's eyepatch again.

"At this point, neither do I. We can find out together. I know a man we can discuss that with," Jean said.

Alcide turned, and looked out into the field. He remembered Suzanne, their daughter, screaming up at a storm, and then Seraphine doing the same on that awful night. He remembered the baby's body, flooded up to the surface.

"We will care for the little grave," Claire said, as if she had heard his thoughts.

"What will your daughter think of moving here?" Alcide asked.

"I am sorry, but I am not sure what that has to do with anything between us," Jean said.

"She will be fine. Suzanne is part of the reason we would like to buy this farm. She has always been drawn to a part of that field," Claire said, pointing to the area where Alcide had seen Suzanne screaming into the storm.

Alcide exhaled, turned to them, and said, "I need only to know that the mare, Bijou, will have a good life. She is not young anymore."

"Of course," Jean said.

"She can still pull a light cart," Alcide said.

"We will take care of her. She can rest," Claire said.

"She has seen a lot," Alcide said.

Claire said, "She has, I know. You have been good to her. You were good to all of them."

"I did what I could," Alcide said.

Claire asked, "Where will you go?"

Jean said, "I am not sure what that has to do with anything between us either."

"It's alright," Alcide said.

"Forgive me if that was too forward," Claire said.

"Not at all. It would be good to return to Paris, and find a place to live out my days," Alcide said.

"But the war is perhaps only ninety kilometers from Paris," Jean said.

"Yes, well, I lived there before, and when the front lines enveloped the city. I will go back," Alcide said.

"So, you will sell the farm to us?" Claire asked.

Jean said, "I have some money. We are told a pension will come to us after the war. I could send more."

"I am sure we can come to a fair agreement," Alcide said. "I will need some time to have someone find me a place in Paris, and to move my things."

Jean said, "Of course."

Claire said, "And you can keep anything from the house that you would like to have."

Jean looked at her, and Alcide thought perhaps Jean would have liked to look around in the house before the offer was made.

"There was a photo. Olivier, the boy, took a photo with your camera of Seraphine chasing Elise. Could I have that one?" Alcide asked.

"It's yours. It is even framed," Jean said, and it was Claire this time who looked like she wished she had been consulted, but she said nothing.

Alcide nodded. *It was time to go back*, he thought.

42

PARIS
1922

"I see," I said. "So, you had given the camera back to them, and they were able to develop the photographs."

"Of course. As I've said, I am not a thief," Alcide said.

"And she gave you the photo," I said, pointing at it.

"There was a fair exchange all around, and I returned to Paris as soon as I could," Alcide said.

"And what have you done here? All this time?" I asked.

"I go for walks. I remember. It is easier to visit the graves here," Alcide said.

I knew immediately he meant those of his wife and daughter, although, I assumed, only one of them was buried beneath those stones.

"Did you ever learn what happened to Olivier?"

Alcide said, "I asked often of people coming through

this way from there, and one day, a government man told me once that he thought I might be referring to a young man farming on a small place in Le Lieu, in Switzerland, who had an old mare that did no work. She only ate him out of hay, and that the nag bites. Also that the man sells wooden carvings of horses and the like. It certainly sounded like them. I hope it's true."

"And Seraphine?" I asked.

"I heard that in the south, in the Black Mountains, and high up, a woman worked as a housekeeper in a large manor house, in a little village known as Labastide-Esparbairenque," he said, and he picked up the photo of Seraphine chasing Elise once again. "A young, beautiful housekeeper with her own horse, a mare, that she rode bareback around the mountains. Simply riding, slowly, and alone."

"You think it was Seraphine?"

"It's said she used to cry in her sleep, and that she called the mare, 'Elise.' That made me think it was likely her," Alcide said.

"What happened to her? Is she still there?" I asked.

"I don't know what happened to her. Only that one day, she went for a ride, and did not return," Alcide said.

"Not even the mare?" I asked.

Alcide put the photo down and said, "The children say that when you are in those woods, if you clap your hands to make the clop-clop of a horse, and then you listen, you can hear the sound of a woman, weeping."

Oh no, I thought. I sat back hard, sighed, and asked, "You're telling me ghost stories?"

Alcide said, "You came here looking for ghost stories, like stories about the Cagots. We are all ghosts now; we are all just stories."

I said, "I wanted to write history, not a ghost story."

Alcide straightened, and looked me in the eye, and asked, "What's the difference?"

With that, I was frustrated, and asked, "Is anything you've told me true?"

Alcide's face set hard, and he didn't answer. I got up, straightened my shirt, and said, "Well, I suppose there is nothing left to discuss. I thank you for your time and hospitality, Mr. Chrétien, and I bid you a good day."

I left the apartment, and made my way to the street. I had come here to learn about the *gens des Marais*, but in that moment, I wasn't sure about what I had been told. Having taken fewer than five steps on the sidewalk, I was nearly run into by a young girl. She ran past me, around the corner, and down the alley out of sight.

A woman walked past me next, stopping as she turned down the alley, and called out, "Viola!" She disappeared into the alley as well.

I ran to the corner, looked deep into the blind way, and I saw no one. Looking up, I considered going back upstairs to ask Alcide about the encounter with the girl and woman, but then decided not to. *After all*, I thought, *what if he isn't up there?*

43

◇◇◇◇

MONTAGNAT
1922

Instead of going back upstairs in Paris, to check on old Alcide, I took a long train ride to Lyon, and then traveled to Montagnat.

Once there, I began asking people who had some mode of transportation if they knew of the Voisine farm, once known as the Arsenault farm, and if they would take me there. Several people answered that they knew exactly where that farm was, but that they would not take me.

One man I asked said only, "But, Monsieur, there is nothing there," before walking away. An elderly couple agreed to take me. The man said nothing, but the woman pointed to their hay cart with her thumb. I walked over, hopped in, my legs dangling, and my cloth bag in my lap. The ride was rough, and the road only got worse. Neither tried to speak to me, until we stopped.

The elderly woman said, "There. Now get off."

The cart lurched forward before I had time to jump down, and I more fell out than anything else. Neither of the couple looked back as the cart moved down the road.

I stood there, my bag hanging from my hand, brushing on the ground. Looking out at the farm Alcide had described, I could hardly believe it.

Both the barn and house were burned to the ground, with only charred framing, sticking up maybe a meter above the ground, like blackened teeth, broken off. The structures were gone.

As I started to walk onto the property, I heard a squeaking sound approaching. Looking to my left, a man was peddling a milk-delivery cart, with one rear tire and a wooden box sitting between two front tires. Milk cans stood, metal and dented, in the box.

"Hey, you there," I called to him, and, since the road was level, he stopped.

"Good day," he said.

"Hello. I wonder, can you tell me what happened to this farm?" I asked.

"The Voisine farm? Where are you from?"

"I am an American, who came here from Paris to talk to the Voisines. I'm a writer for a newspaper, and a friend thought they might have a story to tell," I said.

"No doubt they would."

"Please tell me what happened," I said.

"It burned," he said.

At the end of my patience, I was about to be rude, when he continued.

"The house and the barn burned. Jean and Claire Voisine were both badly burned, but they survived," the milkman said.

"And their daughter? Suzanne?" I asked.

"She set the fire," he said.

"Surely, it was an accident."

"One would have thought, but their daughter took all the animals to safety, before setting fire to the house with Jean and Claire asleep upstairs," he said.

"Suzanne meant to kill her parents?"

"And only them."

I asked, "Where is Suzanne now?"

"I assume she is still in the asylum in Lyon," he said.

"Le Vinatier," I said.

"That's right. That is the one."

I scanned the field beyond where the house had stood, and could not believe Suzanne had tried to murder her parents. "Why did she do that? It seemed, from what I heard, that she loved her mother."

"Who knows? Their daughter was never well in the head."

"What about Bijou, the horse?" I asked.

"She lived out her life with the scarred Voisines, and when that old mare died, Jean and Claire sold the remaining animals, and their original farm. They moved far away. No one has heard from them," the milkman said.

"So, who owns this burned out farm now?" I asked.

"Oh! The Voisines still own it. They sold their original homestead to a young family, but they did not sell this farm that they bought from an old man who lived here alone, I'm told."

"They still own it?"

"And they haven't been back at all. I suppose that they have no interest in it, but they don't want anyone else to buy it either," he said.

"I see," I said.

Both of us fell silent for a minute.

"Well, this milk needs to get where it is going. Good day," the milkman said, and he stood up on the pedal to get the cart moving.

"Good day," I said, and I watched him go for a bit.

Looking up and down the road, I saw no else. I took a couple of steps off the road, toward the house, and dropped my bag in the dusty earth. I walked with the ruins of the barn on one side, and the burned house on the other, but looked at neither. Heading out toward the field, I soon spotted the rectangular patch of stones, smooth and round. Laying flat beyond that, a bit depressed into the soil, was a small wooden cross with nothing inscribed that I could make out.

In the distance, there was a tree line. Tempted to head into the forest, and follow the slope up, to see if I could find the little cave, but I chose not to.

If I didn't find a cave, it would sew doubt in my mind about Alcide's entire story, and now that I stood beside the little grave, I preferred to believe it all.

ACKNOWLEDGMENTS

A quick nod to *Le Cheval*, 1865, par Victor Hugo, and another to the photo often titled *The Horse Trainer*, 1899, Felix Thiollier for the inspiration both provided.

I highly recommend radish slices and butter sandwiches. Perhaps too French for some of you. If you can't do gluten or some such, just dip your fresh French breakfast radishes in good butter.

Thank you to Nylah Lyman and Amy Libby for their help with horse related matters. Any errors in this novel concerning horses and farms are completely my fault, despite their best efforts to help me get things right.

Thank you to Sonia Pareja for her help in improving my understanding of history and culture. Again, any remaining errors are mine, and not hers.

During the research for this novel, I learned that women throughout recorded history, and surely before it, have indeed breastfed animals. It's not an exhaustive list, but, from puppies to goats, calves to monkeys, and, yes, even foals, humans have nursed the young of other species. In some cases, it was to aid the animals, in others it was to aid the women, and sometimes it was ritualistic, but there is quite a bit of documented evidence that this has occurred, and I suspect it must still.

I had quite a time trying to find the right places where I could work on this project, but I found a good one at Uncharted Tea on Congress Street in Portland, Maine. Thank you to Saga, Hayden, and Zo-Zo for suggesting it. I decided, and wrote, Suzanne's fate while sitting one day in Aroma Joe's in Gorham, Maine. The C-Salt Gourmet Market in Cape Elizabeth, Maine is always a good place, too.

ABOUT THE AUTHOR

KEVIN ST. JARRE is also the author of *Paris, California* (2023), *The Book of Emmaus* (2022), *Absence of Grace* (2022), *The Twin* (2021), *Celestine* (2021), and *Aliens, Drywall, and a Unicycle* (2020), all published by Encircle Publications. He previously penned three original thriller novels for Berkley Books, the Night Stalkers series, under a pseudonym. He's a published poet, his pedagogical essays have run in *English Journal* and thrice in *Phi Delta Kappan*, and his short fiction has appeared in journals such as *Story*.

Kevin has worked as a teacher and professor, a newspaper reporter, an international corporate consultant, and he led a combat intelligence team in the first Gulf War. Kevin is a polyglot, and he earned an MFA in Creative Writing with a concentration in Popular Fiction from University of Southern Maine's Stonecoast program. Twice awarded scholarships, he studied at the Norman Mailer Writers Center on Cape Cod, Massachusetts, with Sigrid Nunez and David Black, and wrote in southern

France at La Muse Artists & Writers Retreat.

He is a member of Maine Writers & Publishers Alliance, and International Thriller Writers. Born in Pittsfield, Massachusetts, Kevin grew up in Maine's northernmost town, Madawaska. He now lives on the Maine coast, and is always working on the next novel. For the latest news, follow Kevin at www.facebook.com/ kstjarre, on Twitter @kstjarre, and visit kevinstjarre.net.

Printed in the USA
CPSIA information can be obtained
at www.ICGtesting.com
LVHW090422291024
794794LV00006B/657